NOTHING TOULOUSE

A Fedora Wolf Travel Mystery

STACIA FRIEDMAN

ISBN-13: 978-1500315757

ACKNOWLEDGEMENTS

Merci beaucoup to Katherine Johnstone at *France Guide* and everyone at *Tout France* in New York, Paris and Toulouse for introducing me to the fascinating history, culture and beauty of the Midi Pyrenees.

Mon Dieu,
Donne-moi la santé pour longtemps,
De l'amour de temps en temps,
Du travail pas trop souvent,
Mais de l'armagnac a chaque instant.

Anonymous Gascon Prayer

Part I

We love only what we do not wholly possess.

- Blaise Pascal

1

When someone offers first class airfare to France, accommodation in a medieval castle and enough foie gras to spackle the Palace of Versailles, I don't ponder. I pack. My assignment was to cover *La Flamme de l'Armagnac*, the annual brandy festival, for *Posh*, a glossy travel magazine for people who rarely leave their gated communities. Although air travel these days is as much fun as being stuck in a crowded subway with half a dozen drunks and a hedge fund manager, I've got to admit, "Ladies and gentleman, please fasten your seat belts," is incredibly sexy in French. My name is Fedora Wolf. I'm a travel writer. Welcome aboard.

* * * *

After changing planes in Paris, I landed at the Toulouse Airport. Customs barely glanced at my passport and waved me through, knowing better than to detain a woman in need of a toilet. I was delighted by the reflection I saw in the ladies' room mirror until I realized it wasn't mine. It belonged to the soignée sylph standing next to me, dabbing powder on her perfect nose. I was the unmade bed with raccoon eyes and fright wig. Except it wasn't a wig. It's what my hair does when it isn't happy. It kind of explodes. In every direction. Not wanting to alarm the residents of Toulouse, I wrapped an authentic Hermes scarf around my head, the kind sold on street corners for $9.99, and concealed my sleep-deprived eyes behind a pair of over-sized Foster Grants.

For the next twenty minutes, I stood in baggage claim as passengers snatched up their luggage and embraced waiting family members. Just as I was about to fling myself into a cab, I saw him striding toward me. Tall, slender, walking with the slim-hipped assurance of a matador, he wore an indigo shirt, faded jeans and a pale yellow sweater knotted loosely around his neck.

"Mademoiselle Woof?" he asked.

"Yes, I'm Fedora Wolf."

"Bonjour. I'm Paul Cabanne, your photographer."

He pecked both my cheeks, right then left. I got a whiff of something woodsy.

"My car's outside," he said.

Sweet. My boss was cutting costs by hiring a photographer to schlep me around southern France. Checking out Paul's killer cheekbones, stylishly unkempt hair and deep-set olive eyes, I had no cause for complaint.

"Your baggage?" he asked, looking around.

I jiggled a mini-tote on wheels. It was just big enough to hold a Yorkie or everything I needed for a week in France. Two pairs of slacks, one skirt, three tops, two bras, five panties and several pairs of cotton socks. All black. Plus the toiletries and pharmaceuticals that keep this machine running, as well as my MacAir and electronic translator. My French vocabulary was on par with Tarzan movies. Me-want-hamburger.

"You are not a typical American," he said.

If that was an insult, I was too jet-lagged to decode it. Paul carried my bag as I followed him to the parking lot. It was the last week in October and I wasn't prepared for the effervescent sunlight that gave objects a surreal intensity. My multiple layers of black clothing, which were perfectly suited to fall in Philadelphia, seemed as out of place in Toulouse as a burqa at a wet t-shirt contest.

Paul stopped by one of those tiny vintage cars that I thought had disappeared along with war rations. I peered over the top of my sunglasses. The car's once bright paint was sun-baked to a dull red, rusting around the edges. I'd seen shopping carts with better suspension.

"I can't ride in that." I said.

"I don't understand," Paul said, which is what the French say when they don't want to understand. Against my better judgment and the limits of my health plan, I climbed inside his 1975 Deux Chevaux.

"James Bond drove this car in *For Your Eyes Only*. When I saw the movie, I had to have one," Paul said.

Shame he didn't run out and buy one of Bond's other cars. Say, a Ferrari.

"The seats? You can take them out for a picnic," he boasted.

Swell. I was riding in a 90 mph lawn chair.

"You walked right up to me in the airport. How did you know who I was?" I asked.

"Your shoes. Only Americans wear those." He pointed at my Nikes, then lit a cigarette.

"Do you mind?" he asked, blowing a plume of blue smoke.

Yes, I did. But complaining about cigarettes in France is like trying to cover people up with towels on a nude beach. We drove west on route 124 through the region historically known as Gascony, now part of the Gers Department. Officially, Gascony ceased to exist after the French Revolution when the country's forty provinces, including Aquitane, Languedoc and Lyonnaise, were cut up into one hundred and one *departments*. But locals still identified themselves as Gascon, as if to say to the bureaucrats in Paris, "Change the map all you want. We are Gasonnes!"

From time to time, the Pyrenees poked their purple heads through the clouds. This is France's farm belt, where one can literally live off the fat of the land. And I do mean *fat*. Geese, ducks, rabbits, lamb, pot-bellied pigs and runny cheeses. It is also the Wild West where French is spoken with a guttural twang and attachment to the land runs deep. While there wasn't a cowboy in sight, there was no shortage of cows. Not the sturdy brown Guernsey bovines that dot fields along the Pennsylvania Turnpike, but furry, black cows with wide white bands around their middles. Designer cows. How French.

"This is your first time in France?" Paul said.

"Oh no, I've been to Paris many times."

"Paris is not France," Paul said. He flicked his cigarette in my direction, dusting my lap with a fine layer of ash. "This. *This* is France."

I turned my attention to the vivid landscape of the Midi, the cobalt sky, white-washed farmhouses and a patchwork quilt of chocolate soil, green vineyards and golden meadows. I love Monet landscapes. Now I was inside one. No urban sprawl. No industrial parks. Just idyllic villages with story book names. Castelnouvel. L'Isle-Jordain, Vic Fezensac. But it was all rushing by too fast. I looked at the speedometer. 140 kilometers per hour.

"Could you slow down?" I asked.

"Don't worry," Paul grinned. "I know these roads with my eyes closed."

That's what worried me. He slipped a disk into the CD player.

"Claude Nougaro," he said, "He's the French Frank Sinatra."

I had heard of Yves Montand and Charles Aznavour but not Nougaro. His voice was raw with passion and remorse. Paul sang along in a velvety tenor, swaying this way and that, painting pictures in the air with his hands. The only words I understood were "*Ohhhhh Tulooooouse!*"

Just ahead, a large truck was barreling towards us. The road was too narrow to accommodate both of us. I glanced at Paul. His eyes were closed in reverie. If he didn't pull off the road, we would both be *paté*.

"WATCH OUT!" I screamed.

Paul's hand shot out of the window, making the internationally understood symbol requiring only one finger, then the car swerved off the road into a ditch. There was a loud KA-THUNK. It was my head hitting the windshield.

"*Ça va?*" he asked. "Are you alright?"

The question was relative. I was in a field of sunflowers on a golden afternoon in the Midi Pyrenees with a violently handsome man. The throbbing in my right temple was incidental.

2

A half a pack of Gauloise later, the turrets of a castle appeared over the tree tops.

"*Voilá*. Your hotel, Château Mignon," Paul announced.

The entire village of Mignon was so small it could've fit inside a football field. Every house was constructed of the same ancient cream-colored stone, topped with red tiles. In the center, there was a park with a fountain and a double row of sycamore trees, surrounded by an arcade of shops. From what I could see, Mignon was an affluent community or, at least, one that catered to a clientele more in need of cashmere shawls and crystal decanters than shoe repair and toilet plungers.

There was a small but intimidating women's clothing boutique that featured the same lush fabrics, classic styles and if-you-have-to-ask-you-can't-afford-it prices found on Madison Avenue, an aptly named beauty salon, *La Belle Dame Sans Merci*, next to a pizza shop and a brasserie, *Le Chien Blanc*. In the park, an elderly woman sat on a bench, her head bent over a book. Nearby, a small boy sailed a toy boat in the waterless fountain on a sea of dead leaves.

The entrance to the hotel was so dark, I had to feel my way down the stairs into a dimly lit reception area. A waif with short-cropped white hair, purple lipstick and Kabuki eyebrows sat behind the reception desk. Either she wore false eyelashes or caterpillars nested on her eyelids. A gold cross the size of a small firearm dangled low into her cleavage. A green lace bra peaked through her filmy blouse. Not the uniform one finds at the Four Seasons.

"Bonjour," Paul said, then murmured something in French. *I want to devour you.* Or perhaps. *This is the American journalist I'm stuck with for the week.* I had no idea.

"Mignon is certified as one of the most beautiful villages in France," Nicole recited with rehearsed enthusiasm. "The Château was built in the twelfth century. It has been a hotel since 1996."

Batting her lashes at Paul, she told him that his room was just down the hall, then she tossed a key in my direction. My room was in one of the castle's turrets. There was no elevator. I dragged my suitcase up, up, up a narrow, twisting staircase. It must've been a killer in a suit of armor.

At the top, a door opened to the princess bedroom of my childhood fantasies. Its curved walls were painted a dusky rose. There was a four-poster feather bed, an ancient armoire and sunflowers bloomed in a blue ceramic vase on a table by the window. Next to the flowers, there was a plate of sugar cookies with a welcome note from the hotel manager. I nibbled on a cookie and looked out the window; a panorama of Gascony lay before me, rolling green hills, tilled fields, medieval châteaux and deep woods. Directly below, there was a formal garden with a reflecting pool mirroring the sky.

There's a school of thought that says the best cure for jet lag is to stay awake and adjust to the new time zone. I dropped out of that school a long time ago. Instead, I marinated in a hot, deep tub of Roger & Gallet Bubble Bath, then snuggled under the goose down duvet. My plan was to grab two hours' sleep.

When I awoke, I looked outside. A fog as thick as cotton balls made it impossible to tell the time. I pulled on a turtleneck and jeans, combed my hair with my fingers and headed down the stairs. An elderly woman was at the reception desk. She had the jutting profile of the Hapsburgs, regal on a coin but unfortunate in the flesh. Bulbous nose, prominent chin, a wandering eye, all under a cap of tightly curled white hair, calling to mind a cross-eyed poodle.

"*Bonjour,*" I said, "Can you tell me the time?"

"*Certainment, Madamoiselle,*" she replied. "It's seven-thirty."

"Seven-thirty? Oh good. I haven't missed dinner."

She looked at me quizzically.

"We are serving breakfast now," she said.

Breakfast? Shit. I had slept an entire day. Why didn't Paul wake me for dinner? Not having had any food for twenty-four hours, other than the unreasonable facsimile served in-flight, I followed my nose to the breakfast buffet in the adjoining room. An oak table displayed autumn pears, crisp apples, succulent grapes, scrambled eggs, ham, yogurt, granola, aromatic cheeses and homemade jams, plus an assortment of croissants and pastries. All as artfully arranged as a Cezanne still life. Dare I disturb such a masterpiece? Hell, yes. I piled my plate as if it was last call at the Country Buffet.

I sat at one of the half-dozen tables covered in blue and white checked damask. Hazy light filtered through a tall leaded-glass window. There was a massive hearth guarded by a suit of armor, a menial job for a former knight. An elderly British couple sat nearby, the man's face hidden behind *The Economist* while his wife slipped bits of bacon to an asthmatic pug under the table.

A tall, heavy set woman approached, clutching a dog-eared copy of *Rick Steve's France*. She wore the shapeless, earth-toned clothes and rubber-soled shoes that pass for fashion in faculty lounges from Berkeley to B.U.. The staggering mountain of food on her plate made my selection seem timid. Perhaps she was following Rick Steve's advice to make lunch (and dinner) out of the hotel's complimentary breakfast. Hoping to be mistaken for a French tourist, I kept my head down. To me, the first cup of a coffee of the day is a religious experience to be savored in solitude.

"Excuse me, are you American?" she asked in a Bronx accent.

Damn. My Nikes had given me away again. Without any encouragement, she plopped herself down at my table and stretched out a beefy paw.

"Sheila Schlossberg-Koon. I teach gender studies at NYU."

"Fedora Wolf. I'm a dental assistant from Philadelphia."

That's my all-purpose conversation stopper. Nobody likes going to the dentist or to Philadelphia, for that matter. Sheila, however, plunged forward, going into minute detail about her gingivitis which, from what I could see, required immediate attention.

"I'm here on sabbatical," she said, slathering grapefruit conserve on a croissant. "Working on a book about the Cathars."

The who? The term reminded me of a medical procedure that caused me to cross my legs. Sheila brought me up to date or, rather, back in time.

"In the 12th century, this wasn't France. The entire region, from the Atlantic Ocean to the Italian Alps, was Occitania with its own language, culture and religion."

"But it was Christian, right?"

"Depends whom you ask. The Cathars called themselves Good Christians. But they rebelled against the materialism of the Catholic Church. They didn't believe in war. They were strict vegetarians. Women held positions of power. That's what interests me. A society in which women were equal to men."

"What happened to them?"

"What usually happens to people who believe in nonviolence, tolerance and equality. They were brutally massacred." Sheila shoveled a forkful of eggs into her mouth.

"By who?"

"Pope Innocent III. It was like this. The landowners and nobility of Occitania had a lot of wealth and power. They refused to pay tithes to Rome which they viewed as morally, politically and spiritually corrupt. Meanwhile many Catholic bishops were not just sympathetic to the Cathars, they were followers. So old Innocent launched the Albigensian Crusade."

That rang a distant bell. Something to do with Albinos?

"The Pope convinced the nobles in the north of France to attack Occitania by telling them that they can keep all the castles and lands they conquer. It was a land rush. It was also genocide, a crusade of Christians against Christians. Over half a million people were killed. Then came the clean-up crew. The Inquisition." Sheila sighed deeply. "Shame. It had been a great time for women."

Right. Wash clothes in the river, plow fields and get burned at the stake. When it came to Past Life Regression, I drew the line at indoor plumbing.

"I'm collecting anecdotal information," she continued, "Talking to people, getting family histories, visiting cemeteries."

"People have stories that go back to the Middle Ages?"

Sheila's eyes rounded.

"If it involves money or land, memories go back for *centuries*." She leaned forward and lowered her voice. "Madame Picard, the old gal at the desk, claims she's a direct descendent of the bishop who built this castle."

Huh. That might be a nice back story for my article. *Posh* readers like things to stay in the family, be it heirloom silver, castles or a penchant for cross-dressing.

"How would you rate this hotel?" I asked, hoping to change the subject to something that would allow me to enjoy what was left of my meal.

"A bit too *authentic* for my taste. No elevators. No television. The walls are so thin I can hear everything in the next room. It sounded like they were slaughtering a cow. And watch out for the cassoulet. It gives me the runs."

Fearing a soliloquy on Sheila's gastrointestinal tract, I looked at my wrist, where a watch would be if I owned one, and frowned.

"Oh, darn. Gotta go." I said.

"What's your room number?"

I gave her Paul's room. If Sheila wanted company, it would be his problem.

"Your room is right next to mine," she said, licking her lips, "Are you traveling with your husband?"

"No. I'm here with a, uh, business associate."

"I see," Sheila said, lifting a speculative brow.

I gathered up my things, annoyed that Sheila had gotten between me and a second pass at the buffet. It was 8 a.m. I was too buzzed on coffee to go back to my room or to sit in the lobby so I went to Paul's room and knocked on the door. After some shuffling, out popped a disheveled head, eyes puffy with sleep.

"Eh, bien?" he mumbled and held the door open for me.

I pretended to be fascinated by the view from the window while Paul zipped up jeans, frayed in all the right places, that rode low on his hips, displaying a stomach as taut as a tambourine with a fine line of dark hair running from his navel to his…. But who was looking?

"You missed an excellent *cassoulet* last night" Paul said.

From the lipstick-stained cigarette butts in the ashtray and empty wine glasses, it looked as if I had missed more than dinner. Paul lit a cigarette, sprawled out on his bed, and looked at me appraisingly. I had the distinct impression he was undressing me and trying out different positions. The unspoken invitation to join him hung in the air, along with the ghost of another woman's perfume. Narcissus with a musky edge. That, in itself, was not what kept me from joining him. My libido was clouded by that reptilian third eye. The Past.

My marriage to Arthur Wolf, Philadelphia's most respected and feared criminal defense attorney, had recently imploded. I had been standing in the kitchen, gazing at the contents of our stainless steel SubZero, a habit I found relaxing.

"Fedora, I'm leaving," he said.

"Okay. Bye." I was thinking the moo shoo might be turning.

"I'm not coming back."

"Huh?"

"I'm so very sorry," he said, staring at his wing tips. "It's not you."

Well, of course, it wasn't *me*. Nothing in his face gave him away. Not a quiver of a nostril. Not a flicker of a brow. This was the *look* with which Arthur Wolf, Esquire unnerved witnesses for the prosecution. I stood in the cool white light of the Sub Zero while the man who had vowed to love me until death or premarital agreement due us part drove off in his hand-detailed BMW convertible, leaving me and a tangerine Jetta behind.

I didn't tell my parents or co-workers. Technically, we were still married. Technically, Arthur could come back. When the opportunity to travel to France came up, I hoped it would make me seem more worldly, more interesting. But having a fling with the photographer *du jour* wasn't the answer. Or even the question. What I wanted, more than anything, was for Arthur to come to his senses and come home. Or better yet. To find him waiting at the Philadelphia Airport when I returned, roses in hand.

3

The black macadam road curled like a cat's tail, disappearing into the fog. Visibility was no more than twenty feet. I studied Paul's profile: high forehead, aquiline nose, slight overbite, chiseled jaw. A disproportionate number of my romantic entanglements had been with photographers. I didn't marry one, but I was not immune to the mating call of a single lens reflex. I made a vow. Look. Don't touch. Paul whistled through his teeth, a melody I recognized from the Claude Nugaro CD, *Dansez Sur Moi*. Dance *on* me?

I looked out the window at a white horse galloping in the mist, unable to shut out the ghastly images of peace loving farmers and craftsmen being systematically hunted down and murdered. I knew about the German occupation of France, the Vichy Government and the deportations of Jews. But I had no idea there had been a precedent for genocide in this crushingly beautiful part of the world.

"It's so tragic," I said.

"Quoi?"

"The Cathars. They're all gone."

Paul shook his head in disgust.

"You believe that crap?"

"But it's true, isn't it? Thousands of people burnt at the stake?"

"Yes, yes. It's true. But all the books and movies about the Templar Knights and the Holy Grail. It's good for tourism but it's a fantasy like King Arthur and the Knights of the Round Table or Santa Claus."

"Wait a minute. There's no Santa?"

We turned off the road into the courtyard of Château des Rêves, the first Armagnac vineyard on our itinerary. It was an impressively large Romanesque mansion built of the same pink stone as most of Toulouse, *La Ville Rosé*. The château's walls were almost entirely covered in ivy displaying the colors of autumn, from darkest green to flaming orange, broken only by the lidless stare of shuttered windows. A sleek, low-slung silver Jaguar coupe was parked on the pebbled driveway. We walked through a massive arched gate that looked as if it had been taken from a palace and plunked down in the countryside to make an impression. It did.

"Une *vieille fortune*," said Paul, rubbing the thumb and index finger of his right hand.

"Huh?"

"Old money," he sniffed. "The Revolution didn't destroy the aristocracy. It just relocated them."

He pushed a buzzer. A man who looked as if he had rolled out of a Ralph Lauren ad opened the door. He wore a paisley silk ascot tucked into a cream shirt, a beige cashmere cardigan and tobacco corduroy trousers. His ice blue eyes peered at me out of a deeply tanned face that spoke of summers on the Riviera and winters on the slopes of Chamonix. Wavy golden hair, gone sliver at the temples, curled over his collar in the style of European men of a certain class.

"Welcome to Château des Rêves. I am Baron Guy de Fondeville."

"Fedora Wolf from *Posh* magazine," I said, handing him a business card. He frowned briefly at the card, then took my hand, brought it to his lips. I didn't know whether to curtsey or faint.

"*Enchanté*," Fondeville murmured.

He spoke with a clipped, upper-crust British accent. His eyes smiled into mine as if we had met before - in a brothel. Paul, meanwhile, introduced himself in rapid-fire French, hands buried deep in the pockets of his leather jacket.

"Our vineyard has been producing Armagnac for over two hundred years," Fondeville said. "Other vineyards produce greater quantities. We think ours is the best."

The truth is, I had never tasted the stuff and could barely pronounce it. *ahr-men-YAK*. Pennsylvania doesn't sell alcoholic beverages in supermarkets and package stores. We have State Stores that are big on screw-tops and vintages favored by park bench winos. Before coming to France, I went to a State Store in my neighborhood and asked for Armagnac. A three-hundred pound, gum-chewing clerk slowly ambled to a locked, glass cabinet where a lone bottle sat on a shelf, veiled in dust so thick it might've been there since Prohibition.

"Want it?" the clerk asked, jingling his keys like a prison guard. As a State employee, he couldn't be fired unless he bludgeoned a customer to death and it was caught on video. Even then, his union would back him up.

"How much is it?" I asked.

"One sixty."

"One dollar and sixty cents?"

"One hundred and sixty dollars," he said, snapping his gum.

No wonder I had never tried it. I couldn't imagine any liquor being worth that much unless there was a prize inside. Say, a diamond.

Baron de Fondeville led us on a walking tour of his vineyard, peppering his remarks with geographic references. Studies at Cambridge, travels in the States and familiarity with my hometown.

"Philadelphia? Ah, yes, wonderful film," he said, raising his arms above his head, humming the theme from *Rocky*.

He explained that the Armagnac growing region is divided into three areas, Bas-Armagnac, Armagnac-Tenareze and Haut-Armagnac, each with its own distinct soil, resulting in brandies of varying taste and complexity. He knelt down and scooped up a fistful of earth.

"Smell this," he said, holding the soil under my nose.

I sniffed. It smelled like dirt. French dirt.

"Here in Bas-Armagnac, our chalky soil produces fruity, delicate brandy, favored by connoisseurs," Fondeville said, "We use Colombard and Saint Emilion grapes."

The distillery was a large, open-air structure without walls, topped with a corrugated metal roof, filled with gigantic barrels. The hi-tech machinery, of which Fondeville was enormously proud, seemed incongruous with the medieval charm of the Château.

"It took three great cultures to create Armagnac," Fondeville explained, "The Romans brought us the grape. The native Gascons contributed the oak casks and the Moors refined the distillation process. When you drink Armagnac, you are drinking international diplomacy at its finest."

Paul busied himself with cameras and lenses. He wandered away, then reappeared. I wasn't sure if his absence was for professional reasons or if he had simply heard this all before. Fondeville didn't seem to notice. In fact, I had the dizzying impression he was flirting with me. He stood close. Too close. The intensity of his gaze registered as foreplay. Or was it salesmanship? Armagnac consumption in the United States lagged behind Japan, Germany, Spain and Great Britain. Fondeville seemed intent on seducing the North American market, even if he had to do it one travel writer at a time.

"This is the *alembic armagnacais*, the still," Fondeville said, pointing to a copper contraption with towering chimneys. "The *alembic's* fire produces a very high heat and continuous distillation. The heat forces the wine vapors to rise, then cool and condense, becoming more aromatic and richer in alcohol content."

I followed Fondeville into the Château's cellar, an underground cavern so dark and vast it could have led to the Paris metro. As my eyes adjusted to the subterranean shadows, I felt something warm on my back. It was Fondeville's hand.

"Tell me, Fedora, do you have plans for tomorrow evening? I'm hosting a dinner party for the *Compagnie des Mousquetaires*."

Mouseketeers?

"It's a society which adheres to the principles of D'Artagnan, pleasure over profit," he said, his hand drifting lower.

I put some distance between us and suppressed an urge to kick him in the groin.

"I do hope you'll consider my invitation," he crooned. "It will give you a chance to sample our best brandy and cuisine, and to meet the local vineyard owners who are almost as amusing as the brandies they produce."

"I'll have to ask Paul."

"Paul?" Fondeville seemed perplexed, "Oh, that chap who drove you here?"

"Paul is a very talented photographer."

I had glanced briefly at Paul's website. His work had appeared in French *Vogue* and *Travel & Leisure.*

"Ah, talent?" said Fondeville, "There's so *much* of that these days."

The baron walked ahead of me, toward a row of barrels, stacked on their sides, the color of espresso. He lovingly caressed the dark underbelly of a barrel.

"Now this cask has *real* talent. It is black oak from the Limousin Forest. With each year, the wood ages and darkens, contributing more flavor, color, aroma and complexity to the brandy. It all comes from the wood."

"Don't listen to him," said a short, stocky man in a stained apron and leather cap. "The magic of Armagnac is not from wood. It is from angels."

"Fedora, may I present Jacques Dupuis, our cellar master?"

"*Encantada!*" said Jacques pumping my arm in a hearty handshake. He spoke Gascon, the regional dialect which sounded more Portuguese than French.

Fondeville excused himself, leaving me in the cellar master's competent, weathered hands.

"*Parlez francais?*" Jacques asked.

"A little. Do you speak English?" I asked hopefully.

"When I must," he said in French, then laughed as if this was an old joke.

Jacques's ruddy nose looked like it had been on the losing end of several fights, but his thick neck, broad shoulders and beefy arms suggested he had thrown his share of punches. He absently rubbed a scar that ran across his left cheek. When he spoke, that side of his face was immobile, the other animated. In another man, such disfigurement might have seemed brutal, even terrifying. But Jacques jovial demeanor won out over the side of his face that was paralyzed.

"Tell me about the angels," I said.

Jacques explained that the tannic compounds from the oak barrels caused a partial evaporation of the spirit whenever the brandy was transferred from one barrel to the next. The slight decrease in volume is called *la partie des anges,* the "angels' share."

"The angels take their sip and leave us the rest," said Jacques.

"How do you know when it's time to transfer the brandy to a new barrel?"

"How do you know when you are in love?" he shrugged.

Good question. I liked Jacques. I liked his swagger and his lopsided smile. I followed him to his "office," a wooden table and two chairs under a bare light bulb. He set two tulip-shaped glasses on the table and filled each with an inch of pale yellow brandy.

"There are four noses. I show you. First, hold the glass an inch or two from your nose. Second, raise the glass *comme ça,"* he said placing the tip of his nose inside the glass, "Third, lower your nose into the glass and, fourth, lower your nose again. Then tilt your glass like this to see if it has *les jambes*," he said, pointing to the viscous "legs" that formed on the sides of his glass. "The slower the legs drip down, the better."

Having come of age in the era of Jello shooters, this olfactory ritual struck me as a bit much but I mimicked his gestures before letting the brandy slide around my tongue and down my throat.

"What do you taste?" he asked.

"Uh, vanilla?"

"And pear," he smiled.

Jacques refilled our glasses. This time with a darker, golden spirit. It was stronger but silky with apricot and cinnamon notes.

"The first Armagnac was a young, light *eau de vie*. The second was ten years old, more sophisticated. It is like comparing a girl to a *femme fatale*." Jacques winked. "The older the armagnac, the darker the color, the more complex the flavors."

He brought out a horn-handled knife with a corkscrew attachment and a dusky bottle labeled 1974. He deftly uncorked the bottle and poured out shots of brandy the color of amber.

I sniffed. I sipped. A soft warmth filled my mouth and slowly, subtly, a garden bloomed inside my mouth. I tasted violets, oranges and chocolate. I ran my tongue over my lips and inhaled the bouquet of the empty glass.

"*La queue de paon*, the peacock's tail," said Jacques, "That is how we describe an outstanding finish. It is complex and very, very long."

I felt my face flush. I wasn't used to knocking back shots of brandy before noon. I noticed a bandage on Jacques' left hand, spotted with blood.

"Did you cut yourself?" I asked.

"It's nothing. This knife could cut through steel."

He held the knife in his palm like a fine piece of jewelry.

"It's a Laguiole," he said, "The best knife in the world. They are made here in the Midi. You see, here, on the handle? That is the Shepherd's Cross. Shepherds used the knife as a rosary when they could not attend mass. You should get one." He leaned closer, "A good knife is better than a good lover. It will never leave you."

His blood shot eyes held mine for an instant, as if he could see the empty room in my soul. Or more accurately, the empty bed.

"Where are you staying?" Jacques asked.

"Château Mignon."

"Ah, *bon*. My fiancé works there."

"What does she do?"

I was thinking along the lines of chambermaid or cook.

"She works at the front desk."

I flashed back on Nicole, the concierge with the see-through blouse and couldn't imagine how that audacious little tart could be engaged to Jacques. Then again, this was only my second day in the Midi.

4

While each vineyard we visited that day was unique with its own history, picturesque chateau and fine brandies, after the third or fourth tasting, they all blended into a delightfully fuzzy blur of grapes, cellars and snifters. When Paul and I arrived back at the hotel in the late afternoon, an orange and blue striped van was parked by the entrance. Several young men in dark blue uniforms were clustered at the hotel entrance, talking on cell phones.

"*Merde!*" said Paul, "*Les poulets!*"

The chickens?

"Get out," he snapped.

He all but shoved me out of the car and drove off, leaving me in a shower of dust and pebbles.

"Hey, wait!" I shouted.

The British couple marched out of the hotel in matching Burberry coats, dragging their suitcases and asthmatic pug. Madame Picard chased after them, pecking at their sleeves.

"Monsieur, Madame. Do not go,*"* she begged.

Giving up on the Brits, Madame Picard threw herself at two German men in matching burgundy jogging suits, offering them extra nights, free of charge. In the lobby, Sheila Schlossberg-Koon locked me in a bear hug, as if some great sorrow had befallen her, and yet, there was a spark of adrenaline in her eyes. I have seen it before, people enlivened by their proximity to danger.

"What's going on?" I asked.

"Oh, it's just horrible…horrible," she said.

A young man with prematurely silver hair approached us.

"This sort of thing has never happened here before. *Jamais*." he said.

Sheila released me from her grasp and drew the man to her bountiful bosom. Although such displays of emotion are considered *gauche* to the French, he did little to extract himself from Sheila's fleshy consolation.

"Don't worry," Sheila said, patting his back, "I'm not leaving and neither is my friend here. Right, Frieda?"

"It's Fedora," I said, having no idea what she was talking about or who this soignée gentleman was. Before I could find out, a police officer asked me to follow him into Madame Picards' private apartment just off the lobby. It was filled with delicate antique furnishings. A tall, burly man with bushy eyebrows and walrus mustache stood in the middle of the room, perhaps reluctant to test the doll house furniture with his girth.

"I am Inspector Beaumonde," he said. "You are here on business or pleasure?" His tone was gentle, almost apologetic.

"Business. I'm a journalist."

"*Zhur-nahl-leest*? Tell me, Mademoiselle, exactly what kind of journalism is it that you do?"

"Travel writing."

"Ah, *un journaliste de voyage.*" He made a notation. "You must love your work."

When a man tells me what I love, he is usually wrong. In this case, I hadn't been at it long enough to know myself. But more about that later.

"Fedora? An unusual name," Beaumonde said.

I like to tell people I was named after Fyodor Dostoyevski. The truth is, when I was born, my hippie parents got stoned and threw a bunch of names into a hat. When they couldn't decide, they named me after the hat.

"You are traveling with Monsieur Cabanne?"

I nodded, but I was already wondering what I would do if Paul didn't return. Beaumonde ran through a list of questions he must've gotten from my mother. What was my relationship to Paul Cabanne?

Did I go to his room? Did he come to mine? What time did I go to sleep last night? When did I wake up? Did I see or hear anything unusual?

Beaumonde folded his enormous hands. He spoke in a low, even tone as if discussing the municipal recycling ordinance, his face not showing the slightest flicker of emotion. The Inspector tucked his pen into his breast pocket and closed his notebook.

"What is this about, Inspector?" I asked, thinking back to what Sheila has said about strange noises coming from the next room last night. From Paul's room. Had there been a rape? A robbery?

"The hotel concierge was murdered last night."

Poodle Lady was still there. He must mean Nicole. An elephant squatted on my chest.

"What was the cause of death?"

"That is what I am here to determine, Madame." (I wasn't sure if that was an upgrade from Mademoiselle or a reconsideration of my age.) "Now, I need you to tell me again exactly what you saw and heard from the time you arrived at the hotel."

AGAIN? This time Beaumonde picked my recollections apart with a scalpel. He seemed particularly interested in Paul's whereabouts.

"I have no idea where he is," I insisted for the third or fourth time.

I hadn't mentioned the lipstick-tipped cigarettes and wine glasses. Perhaps I was tired. Or didn't want to get involved in the investigation. One thing was for sure. If the Inspector kept at it much longer, I would confess to the murder. That's one thing I had learned from my marriage to a criminal litigator. A confession isn't necessarily the result of guilt, but the wearing down, minute by minute, physically and mentally of an innocent person by an overly zealous police officer.

Beaumonde finally stood up and handed me his card.

"I want to talk to Cabanne," he said.

So did I.

5

"She was *screwed* to death," Sheila said.

"I beg your pardon?"

"They found a cork screw in her neck."

Sheila made a twisting motion with her hand. My stomach clenched and threatened to return its contents to sender. Sheila's appetite, however, seemed stimulated. She had a wild gleam in her eyes and a smear of jam on her cheek.

I took small sips of water and tried to focus on my plans for the day. I still hadn't heard from Paul, for all I knew he was half way to Mozambique. I didn't want to miss the most important event of the Armagnac Festival, a country fair and brandy tasting that day at the *Bastide d'Armagnac*, the medieval village for which the region and the brandy were named.

Sheila was heading to the fair and suggested we share a taxi. I agreed for purely pragmatic reasons. She had a working knowledge of French and the last thing I wanted to do was hang around the hotel with a murderer on the loose.

* * * *

The bastide's quaint half-timbered houses, *colombages*, reminded me of medieval Tudor architecture. My guidebook backed this up. During the Hundred Years War, when the bastide was founded by the Duke of Amagnac, all of Gascony was under the thumb (and heel) of the British Crown. In one corner of the town square, a horse-drawn wagon displayed an *alembic*, a gleaming copper still. At the other end, two wild-eyed bulls were tethered, too loosely for my comfort, to a wooden post.

A small band, heavy on accordion, pumped out traditional Gascon tunes. Children dressed in red, white and blue costumes performed folk dances under threatening skies. Armagnac vendors and purveyors of local cheeses, sausage and foie gras were positioned all around the square, offering samples. This wasn't Sonoma. No swishing and spitting. I was swallowing and getting sauced while Sheila provided running commentary and translation. My interest was the festival, its history and traditions but the hot topic of the day was the murder.

"This kind of thing never happens here. *Jamais*," said a toothless old woman. "We Gascons die in our own beds. Or sometimes, if we drink too much, in our cars. But murder? Never."

"Nicole was not a Gascon," said a vendor, pouring me a glass of brandy. "Whatever problems she had, she brought them with her."

"Poor Jacques!" another vendor sighed, "First his wife. Now his girlfriend"

"His wife was murdered?" I asked.

"Not exactly," said Sheila. "They're saying she died under mysterious circumstances. Jacques was suspected but never convicted."

"Jacques never had luck with women," sighed the vendor.

It seemed to me that if anyone was out of luck, it was Nicole. I reminded myself that I was within whistling distance of the Spanish border, the Basque region where questions of honor are settled with blood. I couldn't help noticing that every vendor used a Laguiole corkscrew, the same as Jacques' and, from what I could gather, the same as the one that ended Nicole's life.

"They call Nicole *La Marseillaise*," explained Sheila.

"The French national anthem?"

"Nothing to do with that," she said. "She came from Marseille, a town synonymous with crime, drug trafficking and prostitution. The consensus is that she didn't know when to shut her mouth or her legs."

I wondered how much of this was fact and how much was due to Nicole's provocative style of dress. Perhaps she had pushed the envelop a bit too far for rural France, but fashion magazines and rock stars flaunted the heroin-addicted-hooker look. Fishnets and corsets, once the tools of the working girl, were now all the rage in middle schools. The message seemed to be, you don't have to *be* a whore to dress like one.

Some said Nicole and the Baron were lovers. Others hinted at a ménage a trios gone wrong. No one was surprised when the Fondevilles gave Nicole the boot, but their noses were still out of joint about her landing the front desk job at Château Mignon. She doesn't know her place, they said. She puts on airs.

"You see what I'm saying?" argued a woman, "A girl like that does not belong with people of *class*....." She switched into Gascon dialect, leaving me out of the conversation and causing a group of bystanders to erupt with laughter.

From what I gathered, girls her age were constantly streaming through the region, seeking seasonal jobs at vineyards, in hopes of finding a career or a husband. If Nicole was bored with provincial life – and what girl her age wouldn't be - what kept her from running off to Toulouse or Paris? That's what I was pondering when Sheila wandered off to buy a crepe and left me on my own to get more local color for my article.

. *"Canadienne?"* asked a brandy vendor in a green peaked hat.

I hesitated. In the wake of U.S. saber-rattling in Iraq, a cloud of mistrust of all things American was hovering over Europe, especially France. Friends had suggested I wear a Canadian maple leaf pin. But I was brimming over with peace, love and brandy.

"American," I said.

"My son Antoine, he lives in New York. Nine-eleven, such a tragedy," he said.

My new best friend Bernard raised his glass to America, to Gascony and to France's chances in the World Cup. He was a fifth generation Armagnac producer. When I told him I was writing an article about the Festival, he poured another glass and explained how to read an Armagnac label.

"Armagnac does not age in the bottle like wine. The time spent in the barrel is more important than the year it was harvested," he said, "So this 1946 Armagnac that was aged in the barrel for just six years is much younger than a 1990 brandy that was aged for twelve years. *Comprenez?*"

This is the kind of stuff *Posh* readers will love, I thought, although I had the feeling they would drink Thunderbird if it were priced high enough. I complimented Bernard on his excellent brandies and, following his suggestion, visited *Notre Dame des Cyclistes*, a church in the bastide dedicated to the French passion for bicycling.

Hundreds of gaudily colored racing shirts hung from the rafters like heraldic flags along with racing bikes. Bernard said that cyclists competing in Le Tour de France come here before the big race to have their bikes blessed and to pray to be one of the first to cross the finish line. I'm not a believer and have long suspected that God, at best, is an absentee landlord. Be that as it may, I operate on the It-Couldn't-Hurt Principle and, at times, bargain with the Almighty to nudge things along in my favor. Sort of like slipping a twenty to a maitre d'. The Church was empty except for one old woman with a *schmata* on her head, inching her way down the center aisle on arthritic knees, mumbling into her rosary. I slipped into a pew toward the back of the church.

"It's me, Fedora," I whispered. "I know it's been a long time."

I directed my prayer to the ceiling because that is where I was taught that He (or She) resides. Up *there*. Above the racing shirts, rafters and stained glass. Above the clouds, birds and airplanes. Way, way up.

"Here's the deal. A woman was murdered in my hotel. Guess you knew that, right? And this photographer, who's supposed to be escorting me around? He's gone AWOL. I should be on the next plane back to Philly, but then I'll never get another travel writing assignment. Or I can stay and wait for the next body to drop. But it could be mine. What should I do?"

By way of response, hundreds of neon-colored sleeves suspended from the ceiling waved their silky arms. What did *that* mean? Oh, it meant that someone had opened the Church door. I hurriedly concluded my conversation with the Divine and attempted to steer our negotiation to a win-win outcome.

"Look. I really want to give this travel writing gig a shot. So if you can just get me though this week and make my editor happy, here's what I'll do...I'll...I'll volunteer two nights a week in an adult literacy program."

The sleeves hung limp. I took a deep breath.

"And I'll makeup with my sister Ro."

We hadn't spoken in three years. It started at a Thanksgiving dinner over a remark I made about her weight. I know. I know. But I couldn't just sit there while she insisted that a pound of pasta, swimming in butter, was a "snack." There was a thaw and then, for reasons neither of us remembered, a deep chill set in again. Sarah Palin would trade cookie recipes with Michelle Obama before Ro and I were on speaking terms.

"Oh. And one more thing. If you're not too busy. Make Arthur want me again."

For *that*, I'd not only patch things up with my sister. I'd treat her to a Caribbean cruise. But I didn't say it out loud. When bargaining with God, always play your cards close to the chest. The old woman had finally reached the alter and had spread herself facedown on the mosaic tile floor. Whatever intercession she was seeking, whether on behalf of herself or a loved one, it made my requests seem trivial by comparison.

Back outside, the sun peeked through the clouds as the dancing children were replaced by adult couples doing the Gascon equivalent of the polka. A burly man with a scrubby red beard twirled his partner in the air like a rag doll. It was Sheila Schlossberg-Koon.

6

"C'est moi." said a smoky voice on the other end of the line.

"Who is this?"

I knew it was Paul. I was being vindictive.

"I'm in the lobby," he said.

I took my time and made him burn down a cigarette or two. I found Paul slouched in a leather chair by the fire, his face in shadow. He stood. We did the kiss-kiss thing.

"Fedora, I want to apologize," he said. "I had to go home and think."

"Home?"

"To Toulouse."

"You could've told me."

His eyes drifted to Madame Picard behind the reception desk. Paul nudged his chair closer to mine and leaned over. I felt his breath on my skin.

"When you see the police, do you feel safe or afraid?" he asked.

"Unless it's in my rearview mirror - safe."

"Précisément. You are *bourgeoise."*

"Bourgeoise? I don't think…"

"You see this?" he pointed to a split in his eyebrow I hadn't noticed before. "A souvenir from the police. *"*

Paul's story was a familiar one. When he was a student in Toulouse, he did what was necessary to survive. He waited on tables and had a lucrative sideline, selling electronics of dubious origin. In other words, he was a black marketeer. I imagined his apartment in

Toulouse. Futon on the floor, Indian bedspread, posters of Chairman Mao and Che Guevera.

"One night, the police broke into my apartment, confiscated everything and beat the shit out of me," he said, "Now you understand? When I see them, I go the other way."

I was tempted to remind him that projecting past trauma into present situations is called paranoia, but I decided to focus on the issue at hand.

"Nicole is dead. The police want to talk to you."

Paul shook his head slowly from side to side.

"Fedora, there is something I must tell you, but not here."

We went to Paul's room. He perched on the edge of his bed. I took a chair.

"Yesterday was not the first time I met Nicole," he said.

"You *knew* her?"

"She came to my studio in Toulouse a few months ago. She wanted photos for a modeling portfolio."

"Modeling? Was she tall enough?"

Paul held up his palms. "Not all models wear couture. Some don't wear clothes at all. She was young, attractive and had the money. When I saw her behind the desk yesterday, I didn't recognize her. She had changed her hair from black to white. Last night, when you didn't answer the phone, I went to the village brasserie by myself. Nicole was there. She came over to my table, we talked and that's when I realized we had met before.

"So the last place you saw her was in the café?"

"Uh, no," Paul said sheepishly, "She came back to my room."

"Nicole was *here*?" My voice was up in Minnie Mouseland.

"She was upset. She had a fight with her boyfriend. She needed to talk. That is all. Nothing happened. *Rien.*"

"Why not?"

His eyes scanned the carpet.

"Because I don't enjoy making love to a woman who has had too much to drink."

There's a new one.

"Weren't you drinking too?"

"I had only a glass or two. Nicole had been drinking before I arrived and kept going. When she came to my room, she opened her purse and offered me a liqueur. I didn't touch it." Paul scrunched up his mouth. "It was a sweet drink for young girls and old ladies."

"What did you talk about?" I asked.

"I don't remember."

"You're going to have to remember. Inspector Beaumonde will keep at you until you do."

"Fedora, you don't understand. These provincial police are bureaucrats, farmers with desks. If I tell them Nicole was in my room, they will go *cray-zee*. I will not be able to work with you."

"If you don't tell them, it will be worse. They probably found Nicole's fingerprints all over your room."

The color drained out of his face.

"What is this?" he demanded. "An *interrogation*?" He stood up and rubbed his head furiously. "I know who you are. I Googled you. You're not a travel writer. You're an investigative reporter. You write about murder."

He Googled me? I didn't like that. It was as if he had poked around in my underwear drawer. Look hard enough, you'll find things that don't exactly match up. Like a rosary and a vibrator. What really infuriated me was that Paul was right.

7

Until a month ago, I had been an investigative reporter at *The Philadelphia Star,* a pugnacious tabloid that focused on local politics, the dirtier the better. I had worked my way up from covering slugfests in the City Council to reporting on domestic violence. My series, *Men Who Love Women to Death*, made me the talking head on the local TV news whenever some nut job decided to end their marriage with a baseball bat or a gun.

My colleagues were witty, intelligent and politically astute. The newsroom dress code winked at fuzzy slippers and there was talk of syndicating my column. I loved my job. But the mood in the newsroom had grown morose as the economy faltered and reporters took buyouts and emptied their desks, humming *Nearer My God to Thee*. There was talk of terminating the paper edition entirely and just maintaining an online presence. We all knew what that meant. Trimming the staff down to a lean crew of monkeys armed with cell phones who would text in their stories with opposable thumbs.

I was thirty-nine. Too young to retire. Too old to fish around for a new career. My therapist Clotilde, who spoke with a lilting Argentinean accent and wore sumptuous cashmere shawls, suggested I become a freelance writer but I was dubious of any occupation that contained the word "free." I put off my decision for so long that, as with many turning points in my life, the choice was ultimately made for me. In this case, by a ten-year-old with a Glock.

I was following up on a story about a woman who slipped a live cobra down her boyfriend's pants, making him a candidate for some innovative surgery. Cobra Lady lived in a dicey part of Philly known as the Badlands, where it was best to walk fast and keep your eyes to yourself. In doing so, I mistakenly got between a gun-toting middle school kid and his intended victim.

The aspiring Death Row inmate fired. I hit the pavement. A police car came screaming around the corner. The shooter and everyone who could identify him instantly vanished into the brickwork. Nothing induces amnesia quicker in North Philly than the presence of law enforcement. Moments later, an EMT sliced open my Ann Taylor gabardine slacks.

"The bullet didn't penetrate, ma'm," he said, "You've just got grazed. Consider yourself lucky."

I felt anything but. My husband had left me and I was eating cement pie. While a team of sleep-deprived residents stitched up my tuchis at Temple University Hospital, it occurred to me that it was time to reevaluate my priorities.

Getting shot in the line of journalistic duty in Afghanistan could lead to a Pulitzer. The only reward for getting shot in the ass in Philly was an inflatable donut cushion. I had sick time coming and decided to take the week off. My first instinct was to quit my job, have madcap romantic adventures in exotic places and make a million bucks writing about it. Then the oxycontin wore off.

Fortunately, I had a team of experts to help me sort things out. *Dr. Phil, Dr. Oz, Oprah* and *Nate Berkus.* There's nothing like daytime TV to lower stress and lull you into thinking that cutting up your husband's sweaters and turning them into throw cushions is a good idea. Luckily for me, Fate, the patron saint of poor planners, intervened.

"Fedora? I need you!"

It was Sissy Spivak, a former college classmate.

"My travel writer got herself pregnant!" she hollered on speaker phone, "Twins yet! Are you available? It's a one week assignment, but if it works out I could keep you busy."

Sissy was born with a megaphone in her mouth and an exclamation point under her tongue. She had two volumes. Loud and louder. Her marriage to the heir of a publishing syndicate put a lot of serious ice on her fingers but did nothing to soften her northeast Philly accent, which crushed vowels as if they were beer cans.

"But I've never done any travel writing."

"WADDYA TALKIN' 'BOUT?" she yowled. "You're a writer. You travel."

"I don't know. Things are complicated at home."

I was afraid if I left town, even for a week, I wouldn't be there when Arthur *needed* me.

"Oh, that's too bad. I was hoping you could go to France."

Did she say *France*? Of course, I said yes. I wanted Arthur to go insane with jealousy and I wanted to put as much distance as possible between me and the kiddie gangbanger. But being found out by Paul so early in the game was unsettling. I was determined to be a travel writer, even if only for one week. That meant sucking it up and getting the job done.

8

Dinner at Chateau des Reves was a black tie affair. Unless I did a Scarlett O'Hara and got creative with the drapes, my only option was a long-sleeved, black leotard top and a silky black skirt that fluttered around my ankles. I added my Hermes scarf and cowboy boots. It was either boots or Nikes. For the first time since I arrived, I wore my hair down, letting it fall loose to my shoulders.

"Wow," Paul said.

I don't care *what* the magazines say, men like long hair. Paul was doing good things to a trim-cut suit and black shirt with a silver scarf. The effect was what I call GQ Terrorist. His hair was slicked back and he had shaved close. Shame. I kind of liked that sandpaper stubble. He had slapped on some more of that lethal aftershave. I'd bet my Wonderbra it was *Eau Sauvage.*

The drive that had seemed magical in the fog felt interminable in darkness. There are no street lights in rural France. Just the moon and the stars. Whenever headlights came toward us, I shut my eyes as Paul executed an automotive *pas de deux*. Finally, in the distance, I saw a light flickering through the trees.

"Look, a fire." I said.

"Those are the torches leading the way to the Château. It is part of the *Flamme de l'Armagnac* tradition."

We parked and followed the flames to the Château's courtyard where, under a full moon, fifty or more guests were gathered in a haze of cigarette smoke, perfume and brandy. A young troubadour with black curls tumbling out of a red velvet feathered cap wandered through the crowd, strumming a mandolin, singing medieval ballads in a high pure voice that floated and swirled like a magician's scarf. Under an embroidered suede vest, he wore a white shirt with billowing sleeves.

I would've thought he was a *she* if the bulge in his tights didn't indicate otherwise. When he approached a cluster of guests, conversation stopped abruptly as men smiled indulgently and their wives became young girls again, imaging themselves to be the beneficiaries of the handsome young troubadour's ardor.

Most of the guests were stout, balding vineyard owners accompanied by rosy-cheeked wives, snug in their woolen shawls and fur wraps. Members of the *Compagnie des Mousquetaires* strolled about in ostrich-plumed hats and flowing black capes with swords hanging from their waist and blue satin sashes draped diagonally across their chest like beauty queens. Tuxedoed waiters dipped silver ladles into a steaming vat of *eau de vie,* the colorless first brandy of the harvest.

I hadn't worn my jacket and was freezing my bazookas off. I warmed my hands on a crystal goblet, trying to follow the conversation that whirled around me. A waiter passed through the crowd offering glistening black *hors d'oeuvres.* I was hungry but those plump morsels looked like garden slugs.

"Do not resist temptation."

It was Guy de Fondeville, looking *très soignée* in his musketeer finery. A gold wedding band gleamed on his left hand; of course he was married, all Frenchmen are in theory. Fondeville plucked an *hors d'oeuvre* from the tray and held it to my lips.

"What is it?" I asked, prepared to identify myself as a lactose-intolerant kosher vegetarian. I'm not, but the label comes in handy when being served things that are creepy-crawly.

"A French kiss," Fondeville said.

It was an awkward moment. I opened my mouth. The sensation was silky, warm and downright erotic.

"What do you think?" he asked.

I thought that a married man shouldn't be slipping things into the mouths of other women. Fondeville smiled and disappeared into the crowd. When the waiter passed by again, I asked him the ingredients of the *"bise francaise."* I was relieved to find out it was not a member of the mollusk family, but an Armagnac-infused pitted prune stuffed with foie gras. I grabbed two more and washed them down with brandy. I found Paul standing so close to a willowy blond, they could've shared a pancreas.

"Sandrine de Fondeville, *enchantée,"* she said, extending a boneless ivory hand.

So this was the Baroness, Guy de Fondeville's wife. At 5'8", I never thought of myself as short. Sandrine, however, towered above me and was as thin as an after-dinner mint. Her nipples winked through her red silk dress, indicating an absence of underwear. She wore her platinum blond hair swept up into a simple chignon to show off her porcelain skin and features as finely chiseled as Baccarat crystal. Quickly surmising all we didn't have in common, I went in search of a refill.

"Sandrine Lacroix. Amazing," Paul sighed, trailing after me.

"You know her?"

"Everyone knows Sandrine Lacroix. She was a super model."

The name meant nothing. I was a news junkie, not a fashionista. By the time I latched onto a trend, it was in the clearance rack at Marshalls. Still, there was something glamorous about being at the home – a fucking chateau yet – of a real live super model. It occurred to me that Sandrine could be the centerpiece of my article. A genuine baroness, no less!

My mind raced. I'll have to schedule an interview and have Paul take photos of Sandrine in formal and casual attire. Before the evening was over, I would find a way to approach her. To win her over. How could she say no?

9

A bell chimed. Slowly, the well-lubricated crowd flowed indoors. Not inside the château as I expected, but into the barn. Wealthy vineyard owners, producers of the world's finest, most expensive brandy, sat down to dine where pigs had fed at the trough just a few hours before. Under high wooden rafters, linen-covered tables gleamed with crystal, silver and candlelight. The floor was strewn with hay.

I found my place card at the head table next to the Baron. The gentleman on my other side responded to my attempts at conversation with polite smiles. It had not occurred to me, until then, that Paul and I were the only guests who did not live in a château and turn grapes into gold. Speaking of Paul, where was he? I twisted in my seat and looked around, finally locating him, on the other side of the barn, next to Sandrine.

I turned my attention to the engraved menu, listing five courses and as many brandies and wines. Almost every dish contained Armagnac, cream and some form of duck. My conscience and thighs weighed heavily on me.

"How does your wife maintain her slender figure with such rich food?" I asked Fondeville.

"The secret is Armagnac," he said. "It has been studied by medical experts. They call it the Gascon Paradox. We eat a rich diet but we do not suffer from heart disease like you Americans because Armagnac has been proven to reduce heart disease.

"When it was first sold in the 14th century, it was not considered a brandy. It was a magic elixir. They believed it could reverse paralysis, restore memory, heal wounds, even the raise the dead. " He dropped his voice to a conspiratorial tone. "It was the first Viagra. That's why the Muskateers always drank Armagnac before rescuing a damsel in distress."

The Baron stood up and tapped his glass with a fork until the room fell silent. After welcoming his guests, he recited a poem in Gascon, a regional dialect which sounds more like Catalan than French.

"La nouste aigue de bie, Au qui la beu coumn cau...."

Angry shouts erupted outside the barn. Undaunted, Fondeville continued.

"...per ta bielhe si, Ne he pa dou maou..."

The shouts grew louder. Jacques staggered into the barn, red-faced and wild-eyed, dragging along three men who tried, in vain, to restrain him. Jacques snorted, lowered his head and rammed his opponents to the ground. Male guests jumped up to join the *mêlée*. Women screamed, *"Arrêtez! Arrêtez!"* as their husbands, one by one, flew through the air.

"My God. What's going on?" I asked.

"I have no idea," said the Baron coolly, "But my money is on Jacques."

Having grown up around the corner from a joint called Dirty Frank's, I knew exactly what was going on. A drunken brawl. Jacques flashed a knife and emitted a low growl. Blood gushed from a man's hand. Jacques jumped back, grabbed a bottle of wine off a table and stomped out of the barn. Slowly, male guests, covered in dirt and blood and hay, limped back to their tables, accepting the administrations and tears of their wives.

Fondeville took a long swallow of wine and announced, "The poem I was reciting says that if everyone would drink more Armagnac, there would be no wars or conflicts. Apparently, my cellar man has been drinking... but not enough."

There was silence, followed by laughter, spilling over from one table to another, as Fondeville's witty retort restored the mood of the evening to its original effervescence. With a nod, the Baron signaled the troubadour to sing. The music had a soothing effect, conjuring up maidens with garlands in their hair and all the trappings of courtly love. At least, that's what I imagined he was singing about. I didn't understand a word.

"Jacques is a good fighter," Fondeville said, sounding more proud of his employee than annoyed. "In his younger days, they called him Bull Dog."

I wondered if the Baron's cavalier stance was a form of etiquette. Perhaps a man of his stature, his elevated *classe,* must never appear afraid of his employee. The fracas had heightened appetites and thirst. For the first course, *Assiette aux Trois Poissons*, a plate of three different fish patés, arrived with a Château de Laballe 2000 Medaille d'Or Bordeaux.

Next came *Trou Gascon*, a smoked trout, then the main course, *Pintadeau Farci aux Truffes*, guinea hen stuffed with truffles, along with a velvety Côtes de Gascogne Rouge 2001. Along the way, there was a green salad and a cheese plate featuring local goat and sheep's milk cheeses with a *Pont l'Eveque*.

Meanwhile, the troubadour drifted from table to table, his dark eyes holding onto a woman's just long enough to make her blush, then moving on. He seemed to spend an inordinate amount of time crooning into the ear of Sandrine, but perhaps that was to be expected.

"The concept of courtly love was not invented in the royal palaces of Paris, you know," said the Baron. "It all started right here in the Midi."

"What is the song about?" I asked.

Fondeville paused, cocked his ear and seemed deeply amused.

"He is telling my wife that she is the most beautiful woman in all the land and if she will open her gate, he will climb her, uh, tower," Fondeville said. "I'm afraid when it comes to metaphors, these songs tend to be a bit obvious."

The baron turned back to his guests but I remained transfixed by the troubadour's ardent serenade. He never took his eyes off Sandrine while she pointedly ignored him. At the end of his song, he bowed low, removing his feathered cap with flourish. Sandrine tossed something shiny into his cap. I couldn't see what it was. A coin? An earring? Whatever it was, the troubadour brought it to his lips, kissed it and strolled off to serenade a lady fair at another table.

By the time dessert arrived, I was in love. With the Medieval madrigals, with Armagnac and the slow, sensual ritual of dining in southwest France. An envelope of puff pastry was placed before me.

"*Patis Gascon,*" Fondeville announced.

I started to dive in.

"Wait," he instructed.

A waiter circulated, drizzling warm brandy slowly – very slowly – over each pastry in a manner that was incredibly erotic. At the touch of my fork, ethereal layers of *pate a choux* parted to reveal slivers of apple, tender yet firm.

Up until that moment, my favorite dessert had been the hot apple pie at the Melrose Diner in South Philly. The difference was a matter of gravity. After pie at the Melrose Dinner, I couldn't move. After *Patis Gascon*, I could fly.

With coffee came a 1964 Baron de Sigognac Armagnac, a box of Cuban cigars and chocolate truffles the size of golf balls.

"I can't eat another bite," I protested.

"But you must," ordered Fondeville, proffering a plate of truffles. "It is the *specialité* of our region."

He popped one into his mouth, leaving two on the plate. Now they didn't look like golf balls as much as the Family Jewels. Fondeville chewed slowly, lasciviously licking his lips. Okay. I got the idea. I picked up a truffle and took a tiny nibble.

"*Non. Non.* You must take it in your mouth all at once," he said without irony.

Like an ingénue in a porn flick, I complied. A thin skin of dark chocolate gave way to a juicy grape infused with armagnac. When I bit down, it squirted, bitter and sweet, chewy and wet. All together luscious and definitely not for children.

"They are made by *Laporte Chocolatier* in Moissac," Fondeville said.

He snipped off the tip of a cigar, dipped it in brandy, then lit up, his lips sucking rhythmically.

"If you write about my vineyard, you must write about my art collection," he said, "One obsession fuels the other."

Art collection? If that was the case, my article would practically write itself. I'd use the Baron, his art collection, and super model wife to bring the story of the Armagnac Festival to life, to give it sex appeal and glamour. Which reminded me, I still had to schedule an interview with the Baroness. Maybe tomorrow. Whatever was on our itinerary could wait.

God, travel writing was serious fun. And it sure beat the hell out of getting shot in North Philly. As guests stood and moved about, I followed Fondeville out of the barn into the Chateau. Or, more to the point, into *Architectural Digest.* Heirloom rugs, polished tile floors, beamed ceilings, hearths large enough to roast a boar.

"These are my children," he said, gesturing at limited edition prints by Dali, Picasso, Goya. "I never tire of looking at them." We were in the library, a room furnished in a decidedly masculine décor of dark green leather, oak and stone.

"Come. You must see the paintings are upstairs," he said.

I hesitated. With dinner guests in the barn and a half dozen cooks in the kitchen, we weren't exactly alone and yet, going upstairs felt naughty. On the other hand, this was exactly the kind of material I needed for my article, an inside glimpse into the life of a Gascon vineyard owner, a baron no less. It quickly became clear that Fondeville knew not only the history of art, he knew the economics. While his prints focused on 20th century French and Spanish masters, his paintings were an adventurous mix of contemporary, regional artists. The stark modernity of the paintings contrasted with the Louis XV décor.

"Sandrine collects antiques." Fondeville said dismissively, "It keeps her busy."

I noticed that the Baron's accent was becoming more French, less British, perhaps because the subject was art, perhaps because we were a man and a woman alone in a series of bedrooms. He opened the door to the largest boudoir. Hundreds of yards of blue and white damask framed a canopy bed festooned with tasseled and embroidered pillows. I could not imagine Fondeville sleeping in this shrine of femininity.

"I'm not supposed to bring my cigar in here," he said.

Or other women.

"The kings and queens of France slept here," he continued, "This château was the hunting lodge of the Duke of Burgundy before it was bequeathed to one of my ancestors in return for bravery on the battlefield."

I had an uneasy feeling that Fondeville's battlefield was his marital bed. There was a large painting of a female nude hanging on the wall. The figure was sprawled on a divan, her legs spread wide to the viewer.He rhapsodized, "It's all about the line, you see. Delicate, precise, elegant. But you are standing too close. To appreciate it fully you must view it from a distance."

Fondeville sat down on the bed, leaned back against the pillows, stretched out his long legs and beckoned to me. This was one cultural divide I was not going to cross. I remained standing.

"Art doesn't belong in museums," he continued, "You must live with it. Eat with it. Sleep with it. Make love with it."

Fondeville lunged, tackling me around the waist. I tumbled onto the bed; my elbow poked him in the eye. He wrestled his way on top and pressed his mouth on mine. In one swift yank, he tugged my leotard down, exposing my breasts.

"*Merveilleux!*" he exclaimed.

I brought my knee up sharply between his legs. Fondeville howled. Just then, the bedroom door opened and shut. It happened too quickly to see who it was. Fondeville must've heard it too.

"I have to return to my guests," he said, jumping out of bed, passing a hand through his tousled curls and smoothing his trousers. Regarding my disheveled state, he added, "You may freshen up in there."

Fondeville vanished. It had all happened so fast, he went from mauling me to playing the perfect host within a heartbeat. Was that all part of the regular chateau tour or had I unwittingly instigated his lust? I flashed back to rape charges brought on by women against NBA players. Because the women had gone to the players' hotel rooms voluntarily, their claims were suspect. And there I was in Fondeville's bed with my leotard around my waist.

I got up and looked in the bathroom mirror. Not a pretty sight. My lipstick and mascara looked as if they had been applied by a two-year-old. All I had in my purse was Kleenex , a comb and TicTacs. I opened the medicine cabinet and was disappointed to find only aspirin, toothpaste and floss. The cabinet below the sink was much more rewarding. Dozens of lipsticks were lined up like toy soldiers next to eye shadows and pencils, each in its own little compartment. I dabbed on under-eye concealer and some Bulgari *eau de toilette*. Why is it that another woman's tool kit is always more intriguing than one's own? Inside the bottom drawer was a cardboard box of disposable syringes, each wrapped in plastic. Someone was a diabetic or a drug addict.

"*Quesque c'est….?*"

Baroness Sandrine de Fondeville gazed down at me with an expression of bewilderment and disgust. I was on my knees in her bathroom, rifling through her drawers. I needed an explanation and I needed one fast.

"Lost a contact," I said, massaging the tile floor with my hands.

She let out a puff of air, a French gesture that expresses a wide range of emotions – all negative – and stood, cross-armed, while I scrambled to my feet and scurried out of her boudoir. Not the moment to request an interview.

10

Outside Chateau des Reves, guests were milling about in the courtyard, saying their long goodbyes, straggling to their cars. Paul stood alone, looking deeply aggrieved.

"*Allez*. Let's go," was all he said.

The temperature had dropped considerably and not just in the weather. I shivered. Paul did not offer his jacket. He stomped ahead, disappearing into the woods. Between the darkness and my blood alcohol content, the ground felt like a conveyor belt, moving under my feet of its own accord.

"Hey, wait up," I shouted.

I lost sight of Paul and followed the sound of footsteps crunching leaves. Hopefully, they were his. I heard an engine start and quickened my pace, half fearing he might drive off without me. I arrived at the car, out of breath and annoyed. Paul slammed his door shut, as if my presence was a loathsome burden. I stared out the passenger window at the full moon, a silvery pendant hanging in a spangled sky. Let him sulk. I had troubles of my own. We drove in silence for what seemed a very long time. Too long. The car came to a sputtering stop.

"*Merde*," Paul said, hitting the dashboard with his fist.

"What's wrong?"

"We're out of gas."

"How far are we from the hotel?" I demanded.

"I DON'T KNOW!" Paul yelled.

Paul was angry but I was frantic. I needed to pee and we were closer to the Milky Way than to a public restroom. A light flickered in the distance.

"Thank God. A car," I sighed.

We both stared at the light, which was gaining in intensity without coming closer. Long orange fingers reached out, lighting up the sky in smoke and ash.

"Fire!" Paul gasped.

Now I *really* needed to pee. I got out of the car and looked around. We were surrounded by endless fields. Not a house in sight. I climbed over a low wooden fence, walked until Paul and his car were swallowed by the shadows, dropped my panties and squatted.

Nothing happened. It's difficult to pee if you think someone is listening. In the country at night, sound travels. Finally, just as I was relieving myself, I felt a hot breath at the back of my neck. I looked over my shoulder into the eyes of a panting bull and SCREAMED. I ran back to the car, losing my panties along the way.

"It wasn't a *bool*," Paul insisted. "It was a cow."

"How do you know?"

"Because *bools* are valuable. They are not left outside at night."

At that moment, I would've happily traded the so-called glamour of travel writing for my old job at the *Philly Star*. I'll take a pre-teen with a Glock and modern plumbing over a charging bull and peeing *en plein air* any day.

"If you hadn't disappeared for half the night, this wouldn't have happened," he muttered.

"I didn't think you noticed. You seemed very occupied with Sandrine."

"I was being polite. But you? "

Paul's face was inches from mine, but he was hollering as if I was in Cleveland.

"Baron de Fondeville was showing me his art collection…" I said.

"Art? Is that what you call it?"

We were arguing like a married couple when headlights finally came our way, from the opposite direction of the blaze. It was a pickup truck. Paul had a staccato conversation with the driver, then, to my horror, the truck roared away without us.

"Why didn't they give us a lift?" I demanded.

Paul's face was pinched with fear.

"They are going to the fire. It's at Château des Rêves."

11

"*C'est une catastrophe*," said the farmer who drove by at dawn and gave us a ride back to our hotel.

"Was anyone injured?" I asked.

"No, but such a loss cannot be measured in human life," the farmer said, "The vineyard has been destroyed. It will take years to bring the grapes back."

The loss of grapes seemed to horrify people more than the murder of a local girl. There were several theories as to what started the blaze. A kerosene heater had been used to heat the barn for the dinner party. Perhaps someone had forgotten to turn it off. Or maybe one of the torches hadn't been properly extinguished. I asked about Jacques. The last time I had seen him, stumbling and bloodied, he didn't look capable of finding his way home.

"Dupuis? He is gone," the farmer said, hurling a blob of spit to the ground. "*Comme un chien.*"

Back at the hotel, I spied a tray in the hallway. It was 7 a.m. Someone had had the foresight to order fresh squeezed orange juice, a carafe of coffee, croissants and jam. I scooped up the tray and ran to my room. Who can sleep after two cups of dark roast French coffee? I can, but only for two comatose hours. I had to meet Paul in the lobby at noon. I took a quick shower and checked my email. There was a message from my neighbor Adele Margolis, a woman who seemed to have nothing better to do than to monitor the goings on in our little street. "*Two men removed your refrigerator. Thought you'd want to know.*"

Great. Arthur was removing pieces of himself, appliance by appliance, as if our marriage could be disassembled like an Ikea bookcase. And here I had thought that my going to France would cause him to rend his garments and come back to me. But, no, my absence was just an incentive to go on a treasure hunt. My mind raced. Did he bring his lover to the house? Did they do it in our bed? With the blinds open, so that Mrs. Margolis had something more interesting to watch than the bowl movements of her Pekinese?

Outside, the temperature was back to semi-tropical. Paul rolled back the canvas sunroof of his 2CV. Lemony sunshine and the rush of fresh air brought more relief than the aspirin I had taken. We drove over roads that seemed familiar; it was the highway we had taken the day I arrived, except this time we were heading east towards Toulouse.

"After I dropped you off this morning, I went back to Château de Rêves to take photos," Paul said. "Fire is like a beautiful woman. Captivating even when she is destructive."

I could not imagine anyone finding a fire beautiful, other than an arsonist. Paul was enthralled. He spoke of the contrast between the blackened trees and those that were spared, between the charred walls of the château and the parts that were unharmed by the fire.

"The clock tower and part of the house were destroyed but the rest was untouched. The same with the vineyards. It is chaos but of a certain order," he said.

It made me wonder. Was I tooling around France with an arsonist *and* a murderer?

"So, you didn't get any sleep," I said, eyeing the speedometer.

"I don't need sleep. I have a high metabolism and I drink ten cups of espresso a day."

Well, that explained Paul's kinetic energy and moodiness.

"What's on our schedule?" I asked, hoping for a long, sunny ride with minimal walking.

"First, we go to Cordes-sur-Ciel," he said, "It was a fortress built by the Duke of Toulouse on top of a mountain to protect the Cathars."

"Cathars? A guest at the hotel was telling me about them. "

"They had some good ideas," Paul said wistfully. "Except the vegetarian part. I like my *cassoulet*. But they were right about marriage."

"Meaning?"

"They did not believe in it."

"You don't?"

"I married when I was very young. It was a mistake. After my daughter was born, my wife and I decided to live separately. It would've been much better if we had never married at all."

"Difficult divorce?"

"No. That is the problem. My wife is religious. She doesn't believe in divorce."

Hmmm. It's a wonder he didn't kill her.

"So, how long have you been separated?"

"Ten years."

Ten? I twirled my wedding ring. The idea that my separation could last a decade hit me like a tsunami.

"How long have you been married?" Paul asked.

"Seven years."

Actually, seven years, four months, two weeks and five days. But who's counting? I didn't realize I was crying until Paul brushed his hand against my cheek.

"What's wrong? Paul asked. "Your husband, he was unfaithful?"

I nodded.

"*Quel con*," he said, giving my hand a squeeze. "A man who runs from woman to woman is only running from himself."

I appreciated the sentiment, but "woman to woman" did not apply to my errant husband. See, Arthur left me for Vinnie Delgado, his personal trainer at Philly Fitness. What did Vinnie have that I didn't? Let's just say that he made his own gnocchi and leave it at that.

In my heart, I knew that I would not have felt any better had Arthur left me for a Vickie instead of a Vinnie. Not really. In fact, the more I ruminated on the dissolution of my marriage, from the vantage point of southwest France, seated inside the rumbling womb of Paul's 2CV, the more I became convinced that the fault wasn't mine. It was Arthur's. I saw myself among that legion of valiant women – from Ann Boleyn to Mrs. Tiger Woods - who discovered they were married to selfish weasels.

12

We travel for years without much idea of what we are seeking.
We wander in the tumult, entangled in desires and regrets.
Then, suddenly, we arrive at one of those two or three places
which are waiting for us patiently in the world.
– Albert Camus, 1954.

Camus' ode was inscribed on a plaque at the entrance to Cordes. Paul explained that the famous existentialist and other Parisian artists rediscovered the abandoned fortress town after World War II and renamed it *Cordes-sur-Ciel,* a rope in the sky, a jewel between heaven and earth. Situated on a mountaintop at 3,000 feet, the road leading up to the town's entrance was a circuitous route with a multitude of dead-man-curves and steep drops without the protection of guardrails.

Standing on the windy precipice, above the clouds, I could see for miles in every direction. Paul pointed out his hometown Albi to the south, the Gresigne Forest to the west, the Church of Saint-Michel to the north. Below, the Cérou and Aurosse Rivers threaded through the valley like silk ribbons. Whatever dark, disturbing thoughts I had about him were put into proportion by the grandeur below. Yes, there had been a murder and a fire. But there were murders and fires every day in Philadelphia and I never lost sleep over them. I credited my apprehensions to a combination of jet lag, the generic disorientation of being in a foreign country and too much wine. Beaumonde had cleared Paul. Why was I mentally prosecuting him?

Paul took some establishing shots, then we entered the bastide. Its exterior walls were two feet thick and had openings through which to shoot cross-bows, pour boiling oil or hang laundry out to dry. As I walked under the high arch, designed for a knight on horseback, I could almost hear the clip clop of hooves on the cobblestones and the clanging of armor.

"Where is everyone?" I asked, looking at the empty streets and closed shops.

"You're lucky to be here now," Paul said. "In the summer you can't move. Too many tourists."

In late October, most of the artists and craftspeople were gone. Only a handful of galleries and shops were open. I don't like crowds, but nothing makes me sadder than an intriguing gallery or boutique with a "closed" sign in the window. The entire town was only four blocks long. Paul and I agreed to separate and meet at the other end.

The two main streets of the village met in a V-shape by the entrance; at their intersection was an ivy-covered house with a second-floor balcony. Below the balcony was a wide arched entrance, flanked on both sides by a colorful display that, from a distance, looked like flags. As I came closer, the bright splotches of color separated themselves into hand-woven scarves, hats and sweaters. The door was open. There wasn't anyone in sight, just mountains of intricately worked yarn, velvet and silk shaped into fanciful clothing. The hues seemed to be lifted from an artist's palette: Prussian blues, ultramarine, violet, deep umber, burnt sienna, yellow ochre and crimson. No two items were alike. Each was a unique collage of mismatched tapestry, old lace, vintage buttons, ribbons and yarn.

"Bonjour, Madame."

An elfin woman emerged from behind a rack of sweaters. She had been there all along, hunched over her loom. The shopkeeper was dressed head to toe in her colorful creations, giving her the appearance of an oversized, hand-knit doll. It was very hard to make a decision but I finally settled on a filmy cobalt and black mohair scarf, laced with turquoise satin ribbon.

"*Ah, c'est tres jolie.* For you, Madame?" the shopkeeper asked.

"No, it's for a friend." I had Sissy in mind.

The shopkeeper turned to a rainbow of hats and pulled out a burgundy, felted wool beret trimmed with a wide swatch of tapestry. It was the size of a small pizza.

"For you," she said.

"Oh, I don't think so."

Reluctantly, I tried it on.

"Oui, oui, oui," she chirped, *"Comme ça."*

She gave the beret a tug, pulling it to the side. The hat became instantly chic and sexy. It struck me as a frivolous purchase. In Philly, the only women who wear interesting hats are hookers. Still, the beret would keep my head warm in the winter and conceal a multitude of bad hair days. Wearing my new *chapeau*, I walked along Grande Rue, the main street, exploring the tiny fortress town. It had a magical, fairytale quality that could never be duplicated by Disney engineers. Gargoyle monkeys and dogs jutted out of gothic mansions. Masonry work above each doorway indicated the original tenant's occupation. A hammer and shoe for the cobbler. A cow for the butcher. A sword, a shield and a dragon for the alchemist.

Gathering information for my article, I stepped into *Le Grand Ecuyer,* a 4-star hotel with only twelve rooms and asked for a brochure and a rate card. It was located in a former 14th century hunting lodge, displaying one of the more curious facades on the main thoroughfare. The gargoyles on the second floor included a winged woman with webbed feet and a serpent's tail. She had clearly visited the alchemist one time too many.

Eventually, I found Paul in a knife shop, examining a Laguiole, one of hundreds of knives displayed on the walls and inside the cabinets of the small store. The handle had a swirling design of rosewood and ivory with a tiny bee inset in silver.

"Do you like it?" Paul asked.

"It's lovely, but don't you have one?"

"I have many. I collect them."

The man behind the counter wrapped the knife in tissue paper, then placed it in a slender box with the shop's logo. Okay, so it was a knife. With a corkscrew. Same as the one found in Nicole's neck. Big deal. From what I gathered, everyone in France owned one.

"How much did you pay for that hat?"

"15 Euros," I said, cutting the price in half, a habit I picked up in my marriage.

"*Pas mal.* It suits you," he said and took my hand as I stumbled over the uneven stones back to the car.

* * * *

We arrived in Albi in the late afternoon, as the sun was throwing long shadows across the rooftops. We had just enough time to visit the Toulouse-Lautrec Museum and Saint-Cécile Cathedral. The museum was the former palace of the Bishop of Albi, an ironic choice for an artist whose paintings immortalized the depravity of *fin de siècle* Paris. I thought I had seen the best known works of Lautrec at the Metropolitan Museum in New York and the *Musée d'Orsay* in Paris, but I had never viewed such an extensive exhibition of his works. I was struck by the modernity of his style, the large blocks of color and bold lines. Lautrec was only thirty-six when he died. One year younger than I was at the time. If I were to die now I thought, what would I leave behind, besides a husband who no longer loved me and an over-weight cat?

"Lautrec died with a smile on his face," Paul added, "He was a *bon vivant*, very popular with the ladies."

"I'll say. He died of syphilis and alcohol."

In the museum shop, I bought *The Art of Cuisine,* a collection of Lautrec's recipes and illustrations. Apparently, he had been a highly inventive cook who loved hosting unconventional dinner parties in his home in Paris on Avenue Frochot. Lautrec enjoyed shocking his guests, as well as entertaining them. His cookbook included a recipe for kangaroo and roasting a "saint" which I imagine were in short supply in the brothels of Paris.

On Sissy's generous expense account, we dined at *La Table du Sommelier*, a restaurant specializing in regional wines and cuisine.

"Don't scrimp on food and drink," she had advised, "Our readers gargle with Veuve Clicquot." I liked the restaurant's casual, contemporary décor – hardwood floors, exposed brick walls, butcher block tables. It was located in a former hat factory in what had been Albi's Jewish Quarter.

As we entered the restaurant, I felt men's eyes follow me as if I were naked. They do that in France. It's a very direct stare that starts with the eyes, then scans the body up and down like an MRI without the hint of a smile. Back home, that kind of blatant eyeballing could land a person in Motel 6. In France, it's considered harmless. Paul explained, "Flirtation is like breathing. When you stop, you die."

I ordered the Menu Vin Passion, four courses, four wines. I started with smoked salmon and a 1997 Alsace Riesling, then cruised along to grilled steak with mustard and a Pinot Noir. Rounding the bend I polished off a cheese plate with a 1999 Marcillac Domaine de Cros and slid into home plate with crème brulée and a Cotes de Bergerac Moelleux. For a gal who usually takes over a week to finish a single bottle of wine, this was a feat, one I could get used to. When our espresso arrived, Paul pulled a little blue box out of his jacket and set it on the table.

"For you," he said.

I hesitated, savoring the moment. Inside layers of white tissue paper I found a delicate, gold-filigree Cathar cross, not much larger than my little finger nail, on a fine gold chain.

"Oh, it's beautiful. But you shouldn't have."

A shadow crossed Paul's face.

"My absence the other day was not professional. I want you to have only good memories of your time in the Midi…and of me." Paul took the cross out of the box. "May I?"

I leaned forward and held my hair up as he hooked the clasp around my neck. The diminutive Cathar cross added an elegant touch to the ecumenical jumble of amulets already hanging around my neck: a Moroccan *chumsa*, Hebrew *chai,* Saint Anthony medallion, and Santeria beads. When it comes to the Evil Eye, I don't take chances.

"When did you buy this?" I asked.

"While you were buying your hat in Cordes-sur-Ciel."

"And you kept it a secret all this time?"

"*Mais oui.* It's only been a few hours. A real secret is one you keep for years."

Actually, no. A real secret is one you keep from yourself and pay a therapist two hundred bucks an hour to excavate.

* * * *

After dinner, we wandered through the streets of Albi, delightfully tipsy. I felt as if I were floating just above the pavement. Paul lit up a cigarette. I thought how good it smelled, the tobacco smoke mingling with the autumn night air.

"Has your family always lived here in Albi?" I asked.

"On my father's side, they've been here forever, going back to the Cathars. My mother's family came from Algeria in the 1960s."

That explained his olive skin and gazelle eyes.

"You are like me," I said. "A mixed breed."

Paul shot me a confused look.

"*Un mélange,* a combination of nationalities," I said.

"*Oui, oui.*"

"Does your daughter look like you?"

"No, she takes after her mother. Light hair, light skin, blue eyes. But she has my temperament."

"Meaning?"

Paul wagged his head from side to side and growled like a dog refusing to relinquish a favorite sock.

"Stubborn, independent, opinionated. But underneath…she is an angel."

Hearing Paul express his love for his daughter made me go all gooey inside. I wanted to kiss him. Instead, I asked about the old building across the street from us.

"Is this a historic place?"

"Very important," he smiled, "It is *Lycée Lapérouse,* my high school."

I tried to envision Paul as a teenager.

"Were you a good student?"

"I was terrified of my teachers, afraid of failing my exams, desperately in love with a girl who didn't know I existed."

"That's hard to believe."

"I was shy," he said, adding, "Sometimes I still am when I am not sure if the interest is mutual."

13

"Would you like to see what I shot today?" Paul asked.

If it meant getting out of bed, I was in no hurry. We were in Paul's room at our hotel in Mignon. I was as relaxed as a de-boned duck, glazed in its own juices. There had been no mad ripping off of clothes, just a slow, sensual dance between two consenting adults who knew all the steps. Why had I broken my rule about keeping my distance? I could blame it on the wine, the moonlight or the topaz glint in Paul's eyes. But more to the point, it was Arthur taking the SubZero. If he could brazenly take what he wanted, so could I.

Paul hopped out of bed, affording me a highly pleasurable view, and returned with his laptop. He set it on my lap and started a slide show.

"Tell me honestly what you think," he said, disappearing into the bathroom.

There were close-ups of architectural details in Cordes-sur-Ciel and the Saint Cecile Cathedral in Albi. Paul's photography was as artful as his lovemaking. But, whoa. What was this? A close-up of a woman. Her cheeks were flushed, eyes shining. It was *me*. I hate being photographed. My phobia goes back to those sweaty photographers who came to my elementary school and tried to make me smile. In Paul's photos, however, I appear to be one of those carefree young women who cavort in perfume ads. Radiant, shimmering, adored. I clicked to the next photo. Me again. And again! He even had shots of me in my new beret. How had he done that without my knowledge?

"Hey, you're not being paid to take photos of me."

"Did I?" he said from inside the bathroom, "Ah, well, sometimes my camera has a mind of its own."

I continued clicking through the images, going back in time. Photos of Château des Rêves appeared, focused on small details. A white cat sleeping in a patch of sunlight. Grapes ripening on the vine. Giant oak casks. Easy to see why Sissy had hired him. Paul wasn't just another local photographer; he was an artist. I wanted to start the slide show over. I clicked. Nothing happened. I clicked again and again.

An image appeared on the screen, but not the one I wanted. This one was of a young woman lying on a bed, eyes glazed, lips parted. I saw a lithe torso, slender legs, pale breasts and a Toulouse cross. Nicole! These weren't studio shots. I recognized the headboard, the bedspread, the lamp in the background. The photos had been taken here, in this hotel room, in this bed.

I slammed the laptop shut, jumped out of bed and starting grabbing up my clothes. Paul emerged from the bathroom in a cloud of steam, a white towel wrapped low on his brown hips.

"What's wrong?" he asked.

"I've got to go back to my room. I won't be able to sleep if I stay."

He pulled me close and bit my earlobe.

"*Eh, bien.* We don't have to sleep," he murmured.

There was that smile again. This time it scared me, along with his new Laguiole knife resting innocently on the bedside table. I thought of all the charming psychopaths who seduced their victims, then chopped them up into little pieces.

"No, really, I have to go," I insisted.

Paul kissed me lightly on both cheeks. Not exactly the actions of a serial killer. I ran to my room, bolted the door and dumped the contents of my handbag onto the bed, sifting through maps, brochures and business cards until I found the one I needed. I dialed the number on the card.

"Inspector Beaumonde?"

14

The next morning, Beaumonde met me in the hotel lobby wearing the aggrieved expression of a civil servant who must entertain the imaginings of fools, at least until his pension kicked in. I looked around for the fire power that usually accompanies the take-down of a "person of interest" back in Philly. There was no one except a German family dawdling over breakfast, Madame Picard fussing about the buffet and her husband sorting mail behind the reception desk. I hoped Beaumonde's men already had the hotel staked out with sharpshooters on the roof or hiding in the bushes.

"Paul hasn't had breakfast yet," I said. "Are you going to his room? I don't want him to see me with you."

Beaumonde held up his enormous palms and patted the air.

"Please wait here. I will come back to speak with you after I have met with Monsieur Cabanne. Enjoy your breakfast."

Enjoy my breakfast? Impossible. Some people eat when their nervous. Me? I had enough squirrels inside my stomach to lose a full size by noon. An ominous THUD was coming from the stairwell. It sounded like the scary part of *Fantasia* where all the brooms start marching. I thought someone was dragging a heavy suitcase (or a dead body) down the stairs, but no, it was Sheila.

"Bone jar," she said.

"I beg your pardon?"

"*Bone jar*. Good morning. Had breakfast yet?"

"Uh, no, I…"

"C'mon let's grab a table."

Sheila threw a massive arm around me and steered me toward the dining area. Watching her pile her plate high with eggs and cheese and pastries made me woozy. I had coffee and a few orange wedges.

"Aren't you eating?" she asked. "It comes with the room, you know."

"My stomach's upset. Probably something I ate last night."

Namely, Paul.

"They'll kill ya with the rich food here," Sheila commiserated, smearing a thick coat of butter and jam on a croissant. She cast a critical eye at the buffet table. "Should've brought bagels. I've had lox and bagels in Peru for Chrissake. You know why they don't have them here? Because this was Vichy France. They don't want to remember what they did or who they did it to. If they served bagels it would be an acknowledgement. Jews exist."

"Maybe there just aren't any Jewish bakeries in the region."

Sheila paused, mid forkful. "So, they could get them frozen from Paris. I'm just sayin." Then she looked at me funny, like I had put my clothes on inside out. "….did you sleep well last night?" she asked.

I had forgotten. Sheila's room was next to Paul's. Was she awakened by my love cries, which, I am told, rival the mating call of a wildebeest.

I mumbled into my coffee. My third cup that morning.

"I can't find my watch," she said. Bits of yolk flecked her lips. "I always take it off at night and leave it next to the bed. This morning, it wasn't there. Whaddya make of that?"

"Huh?"

"The thing is, it doesn't work half the time. It's an antique, an Elgin from the 1940s. It belonged to my mother. You know, one of those old fashioned watches with the black cord band and diamonds?"

I nodded sympathetically, but I wasn't paying attention. I was focused on the two movies running simultaneously inside my mental MultiPlex. In one, Paul's naked body moved languidly in time with mine, his eyes smoky with desire.

Playing in Cinema Two, *Psycho*! I saw Paul's lust for Nicole turn violent, his hands enclosing her slender neck, squeezing the life out of her, perhaps playing the erotically charged "chocking game." Then, in the predawn hours, he carries her in his arms like a child, out of his room, through the garden and dumps her behind the hedge like a dead cat. My stomach contracted, filling my mouth with bile. I jumped up, ran to the closest restroom and got down on my knees.

The absurdity of my situation struck me. What the hell was I doing in France? I longed for my own bed and my husband. Arthur still loved me. He was just going through male menopause. I had to be patient, a trait I sorely lacked, which made it all the harder to wait for Inspector Beaumonde. Eventually, he lumbered back into the lobby and guided me to a quiet corner.

"Did you arrest Paul Cabanne?" I asked.

"*Madame,* if I were to arrest every man who took pictures of naked women, or who liked to look at such pictures, I would have to arrest all the men in France…and perhaps some of the women."

"But the photos of Nicole…"

Beaumonde cleared his throat noisily.

"I have spoken with Monsieur Cabanne and I am satisfied with his explanation."

Beaumonde's tone was brusque and the implication clear. If the Chief Inspector was satisfied, who was I to disagree? I had prepared myself for The Worst, Paul being led away in shackles. But the worst is never what we imagine, it is that which we cannot conceive.

Paul was not a suspect. He was a talented, intelligent, handsome man and a tiger in bed. Instead of lighting candles for prayers answered, I called the cops on him. I was so embarrassed I wanted to jump on the next plane home. I reminded myself, I wasn't on vacation, I was on assignment. Journalists, like soldiers, do not wimp out.

Breakfast, which I hadn't eaten, was over and I was famished. An ornamental bowl filled with green apples was on the reception desk. Madame and Monsieur Picard were elsewhere. I grabbed a big, juicy one and was almost down to the core when Paul stormed through the lobby, glared at me for one furious moment, zipped his jacket, then went outside. I had no choice but to follow him out to the car, both of us avoiding eye contact like two people who had met at a drug deal gone wrong. Paul floored the gas so hard that the wheels spun before gaining traction, tearing out of the village with a high-pitched whine.

I kept my nose in a guidebook provided by the Midi Pyrenées Tourism Office. We were going to Lectoure, twenty minutes north. The big deal there was a plant called woad in English, *pastel* in French. When it blooms in spring, woad forms a bright yellow carpet around Lectoure. But it isn't the flower that makes the plant a valuable commodity. It's the indigo pigment extracted from its leaves. During the Renaissance, woad was the cash crop of the Midi, creating immense wealth for those who lived in the "Blue Triangle" of Toulouse, Carcassonne and Albi. The plant produced the royal blue fabrics worn exclusively by the French court and financed the construction of "*pastel* palaces," the grand mansions of woad merchants in the 15th and 16th centuries. When synthetic dyes replaced woad, it became just another weed.

We pulled up to Bleu de Lectoure, an art gallery and workshop housed in a former tannery, a long two-storey beige building with blue wooden shutters. There was a car parked outside the building, the same shade of blue. The gallery and workshop was run by Denise Lambert whose husband Henri first saw the potential for producing natural dyes from woad using modern technology.

"In the beginning, we were interested in woad as a pigment for artists, but we expanded, producing natural clothing, home products, house paints and textiles for the European market," Denise explained. Her biggest client was AirFrance who used Bleu de Lectoure's natural dyes for the interior décor of aircraft.

"We also have a shop in Toulouse named La Fleurée de Pastel," Denise said, "If you go there, be sure to visit Hotel Delfau, a palace built by a woad mogul in 1495."

I found myself humming Bob Dylan's *Tangled Up in Blue* as I examined the items for sale in the gallery: filmy scarves that looked as if they had been snatched from a piece of sky, denim shirts in the style worn by Napolean's soldiers, square cubes of blue soap, necklaces, sealing wax and a blue feather quill pen. I bought a silk scarf for my mother and necklaces for my sisters. As a salesgirl carefully wrapped my purchases in blue tissue paper, she murmured in French, "Your husband is very handsome."

"He's not my husband," I replied.

Her eyes drifted to my wedding ring.

"*Ah? Bon,*" she said with a conspiratorial smile.

*   *   *   *

Our next stop, Moissac, was more of a challenge. There was no one to run interference between Paul and me. He hid behind his cameras while I wandered around the Saint-Pierre Abbey and the Moissac Cloister, a World Heritage site, which had been home to Benedictine monks for over a thousand years, until it was taken over by the Augustinians. The French Revolution had turned the cloister into an army barracks and soldiers had used the magnificent colonnade for target practice, shooting the heads off of irreplaceable medieval carvings of saints and martyrs. One regime's treasure, the next regime's amusement park.

Guilt was gnawing at me. I wanted to apologize to Paul, if only to lower the animosity that hovered between us. But I wasn't ready to kiss and makeup. Just because the Inspector gave him a free pass, didn't mean he wasn't somehow involved in Nicole's murder or, perhaps, holding back crucial information.

I decided to self-medicate. I saw a dark brown awning with gilt lettering, *Laporte Chocolatier* and, upon entering, was immediately assaulted by the intoxicating aroma. This was where Fondeville had said that they made those addictive Armagnac-filled chocolates. I bought a dozen; the price was steep but worth it. I figured the exquisitely crafted chocolates would defuse the tension between Paul and me. Or, at least, take me to my Happy Place.

I found Paul sitting on a bench outside the abbey engaged in conversation with a petite brunette. She wore a starched white shirt and black skirt; I figured her for a waitress on break. As I approached, her eyes flickered in my direction, then back to Paul.

"*Bonjour*," I said to her, "I'm Fedora Wolf."

"My American client," Paul muttered condescendingly. His client? Hmm. The girl twisted a strand of hair with her fingers and said something under her breath. Paul stood up and swung his camera bag over his shoulder. We walked to his car. Before he turned the key in the ignition, I held out the chocolates. Paul brushed them away.

"I'm diabetic," he said and drove back to our hotel without another word.

15

"Your hormones are out of whack," said Sissy who was going through The Change and credited hormones with every evil from hot flashes to weapons of mass destruction. She reasoned, perhaps correctly, that by pharmaceutically lowering men's testosterone levels we could put an end to war. It would also put an end to the Super Bowl, a small price to pay for world peace.

"Listen, here's what you do," she said, "Take a break from Mr. Hot Stuff. Go get your hair done, have a manicure and a massage. You're in France, for chrissake. A day of beauty will help you relax and give you great material for your article. Just put it on the expense account."

We were talking on Skype. Apparently, I looked so bedraggled, she was willing to spring for a make-over.

"Thanks, Sissy."

"Don't thank me. It's all part of the job. Your predecessor got herself waxed and polished at every spa from Paris to Kuala Lumpur."

Part of the job, huh? At *The Daily Star*, the only perk, besides free pizza once a week and the occasional box of donuts, was my weekly scavenger hunt through the box of books, CDs and DVDs next to the Arts and Entertainment editor's desk that had a hand-written sign, "Free to good home." The idea of putting a spa or beauty salon on an expense account made me giddy.

Since my French depended on hand gestures, my electronic translator and the kindness of strangers, I walked across the village square the next morning to make an appointment in person at *La Belle*

Dame Sans Merci rather than risk a phone call. A bell jingled as I opened the door to a small reception area, smelling of hairspray. The walls were the palest pink, the carpet was maroon. Mirrored chrome shelves displayed hair and skin products, along an assortment of tortoise shell barrettes, head bands and rhinestone encrusted hair-combs.

There was no one behind the desk and I was about to leave when a high-pitched voice sang out *bonjour,* followed by a woman in a starched pink smock with the name Antoinette embroidered in red above her left breast. Her eyes danced with happiness and she clasped her hands as if she could hardly contain her joy. Either she mistook me for Someone of Consequence or saw in me a chance to finally put into action all she had learned at beauty school.

"I want...." My hands flew up to my hair as I pantomimed a wash and blow dry.

"*Oui, oui.*" Antoinette cried.

"And also....*un massage?*"

She presented me with the salon's menu of services. Without much persuasion, I signed up for the whole shebang, the Champagne Package: hair styling, facial, exfoliation, manicure and pedicure. She opened her appointment book and, after much flipping of pages back and forth, gave me the option of commencing immediately or coming back the following week. God willing, I'd be home then. I had planned to visit an archeological site that morning but, putting myself in the well-heeled shoes of *Posh* readers, I figured they'd be more interested in French beauty rituals than Greco-Roman ruins.

"Follow me, *s'il vous plait*," said Antoinette, pushing aside the opaque pink curtain that separated the reception area from the inner workings of the salon. She ushered me into *une chamber privé* that contained a padded maroon client chair and massage table. She took my jacket and helped me into a wrap-around smock.

I sat in the chair while Antoinette fluttered about, assembling her creams, lotions and paraphernalia. Unlike most American beauty salons, where everything and everyone is in full view, including clients with aluminum foil sprouting from their head like an extraterrestrial, the salon was as discrete as a lap dance club, a maze of private cubicles and curtains. What happened in *La Belle Dame Sans Merci*, stayed there.

"We start with facial," Antoinette said, reclining my chair. She placed cotton balls soaked in something cool on my eyelids and turned on a machine that directed puffs of steam at my face.

"Five minutes," she said and padded away.

Lying there with my eyes closed, I became aware of an herbal aroma with each warm breath of steam. Verbena, lavender, mint? Slowly, the tension in my face, which I hadn't noticed before, started to relax. I, Fedora Wolf, whose last facial was a $2.95 St. Ives Clay Mask, was finally participating in the ancient beauty rituals dating back to Madame de Pompadour and before. Think about it. There had to be an ambitious cave woman, a Cro-Magnon Mary Kay, who first discovered the youthful benefits of slathering her face with mud and set up the first distributorship.

I was practically asleep when Antoinette tip-toed back and began gently massaging my face with an almond-scented cream. Do with me what you will, sang my heart, as her astute finger-tips tapped, stroked and played the Brandenburg Concerto up and down my forehead, cheeks and neck. Many lotions and unguents later, Antoinette set about massaging my hands and arms until they were as limp as jellyfish. Then she guided me to the massage table and turned on a tape player. Tropical birds sang, monkeys chattered, rain fell in gentle cascades. I was in an electronic rain forest.

For the next hour, Antoinette rubbed and pummeled my body with sesame oil and exfoliated my skin with sea salt, expertly locating and loosening muscle knots that had been in spasm since my husband had walked out the door with our Kitchen Aid mixer. I was so relaxed she could've braided me into a challah.

"I will be back in ten minutes," she whispered, dimming the lights and leaving me wrapped in a cocoon of warm, herbal scented towels.

The music transported me. Amazonian parrots, with a great flapping of their blue and yellow wings, soared high above the jungle, taking my anxieties and fears with them. Arthur Wolf and all the other stress that was waiting for me back home, were washed away in a soothing downpour. I imagined monkeys in the tree tops playfully hurling coconuts on my husband's head. Crack! Thunk! Splunk! And why had I anguished so over Paul Cabanne? I was a babe, a svelte nymph, a hottie. As my girlfriends used to say, "*NEXT!*"

In this dreamy state, I vaguely heard the jingle of the front door bell, hushed voices, the rustling of curtains. After what seemed like much more than ten minutes, Antoinette popped back in the room, turned up the lights and switched off the jungle tape. Her cheeks were flushed and she blinked her eyes rapidly.

"*Allons, allons,*" she said, helping me off the table.

My legs were jello. Antoinette seemed impatient as she steered me back to the chair and lowered my head to the sink.

"Another client?" I asked.

"*Oui, oui, oui,*" she gushed. "A very important client."

My neck muscles tightened. If the other customer is a big cheese, what am I? Velveeta? After rinsing off the shampoo, Antoinette squeezed the excess water out of my hair, then massaged in something that smelled like fruit salad.

"What is that?" I asked.

"Glacé."

Ice cream? Not quite. It was a product to make my hair silky and give it a high shine. She combed out my mane, patiently untangling knots as tightly woven as dreadlocks, then picked up a scissors. My heart stopped. There are people who know how to split atoms. There are people who know how to jump-start hearts that have stopped beating. But in my experience, there is hardly anyone who knows how to cut naturally curly hair. At least that's what I decided at the tender age of eight when a zealous beautician at Kids Cuts chopped off my hair to chin length when it was wet, not realizing that when it dried and shrank, I would look like Richard Simmons.

Antoinette quickly calmed my fears by demonstrating that she would only trim the ends and give my hair what she called "*forme.*" I began breathing again and let myself be hypnotized by the "zip, zip, zip" of her scissors as tiny clumps of hair (pieces of *me!*) fell to the floor. She spritzed on some more nifty smelling product, ran her fingers through my hair and set up heat lamps – blow driers turn curly hair into shredded wheat – and left me with a well-thumbed copy of *Marie Claire.*

My attempt to glean advice from the magazine's fashion columnist was distracted by the conversation on the other side of the partition. Their voices rose and fell steady like a church choir. I only caught a word here and there, but from the rhythm of their sentences, I sensed that the subject had nothing to do with graying hair or dry skin. It had the sound of a confessional, the client unburdening herself of secrets and sorrows, Antoinette clucking in empathy. Their conviviality was getting to me. Antoinette hadn't asked me anything about myself, other than my preference for mint or lavender shampoo. Now she was gaily chattering away, neglecting me and letting my Champagne Package fizzle into Gatorade.

My hair was almost dry and, I had to admit, it looked amazing, falling around my face in glossy swirls like the models in *Marie Claire.* But what about my manicure?

"Antoinette?" I called, sticking my head outside the curtain.

I heard her murmur apologies to her client, before toddling towards me with pursed lips.

"Oui, mademoiselle?"

I felt foolish and petty.

"Ou est le toilette?" I asked.

"Ah, the restroom is there," she said, pointing to a door marked *dames* at the end of the corridor.

"Merci."

On my way back from the ladies room, I loitered outside the *chamber privé* where Antoinette was fawning over her VIP. As I suspected, they weren't talking moisturizers. The client was debating whether to leave her husband; she worried about starting over at her age. Antoinette assured her she was still young and *"tres jolie."* I didn't understand every word but I caught the drift. She was having an affair. Antoinette congratulated her.

"Today, a woman can live like the kings of France. Do what you want, whatever makes you happy," she said.

I heard a ripping sound, followed by a horrific scream. I pulled back the curtain, expecting to find a scissors jabbed into the client's aorta. Antoinette stared back at me, eyes popping out of her head, her mouth opening and closing like a blow fish. Dangling from her hand was a hairy strip of gauze. It wasn't a murder in progress. It was a bikini wax. I couldn't see the client's face, just two white thighs spread wide. Oops! I tugged off the smock, grabbed my jacket, threw a pile of Euros on the counter and ran out the door. Outside the salon, a silver jaguar sparkled in the afternoon sun. Oh, my God! The half-waxed twat I just saw belonged to Baroness Sandrine de Fondeville.

16

I was still snickering over my gynecological glimpse of the Baroness when Sheila ambushed me in the hotel parking lot.

"What perfect timing," she chortled. "The taxi will be here any minute."

Talking to Sheila was like walking into the second act of a play in progress or, for that matter, like talking to my mother. Her agenda always came first, then the details. Sheila's agenda that afternoon was to get me to go with her to the foie gras market in Eauze.

"You don't want to miss this," she wheedled, "It's something you won't find *anywhere* else in the world."

My gut told me that Sheila just wanted someone to split cab fare, but I went along with her anyway. To me, foie gras was like gefilte fish, something I could eat on rare occasions, as long as I didn't think too hard about how it was made. I had a great haircut and didn't want to waste it working on my laptop in my hotel room. Sheila, bless her academic soul, had researched all the particulars.

"There are outdoor markets throughout the Midi Pyrenées, every day of the week including Sunday," she said, "But they only have foie gras in Eauze on Thursdays."

"Aren't you bothered by the cruelty of it?" I asked. "I've seen ducks and geese here sitting on lawns like decoys. They're so fat, they can't walk."

"They only force-feed them for the last few weeks of their lives. It's not so different from the way American farmers fatten up their cattle and chickens with hormones."

Our taxi driver turned around.

"To get the real foie gras is a complicated process," he injected, "It takes a lot of love."

It would take more than love to get me to try any of the fatty livers displayed in the marketplace. Brightly-colored, striped canvas awnings ringed the town square, Place d'Armagnac. Locals and tourists swarmed the dozens of kiosks, their tables piled high with glass jars and metal containers brimming with duck and goose liver. That alone, wouldn't have been so bad, but several vendors displayed whole white livers, the size of footballs, in clear plastic bags. Call me squeamish, I think the place for internal organs is the morgue. The first time I saw a cow's tongue in my mother's kitchen I screamed for hours.

Feeling a wave nausea coming on, I wandered over to the truffle vendors. Although these lumps of fungus didn't look particularly appetizing, I thought they might provide more of a "story" than the foie gras.

"What does it taste like?" I asked a vendor.

"Like the earth and the sky," he said, holding up what looked like a lump of coal. "We call them *Diamantes Noir.*"

Black diamonds, huh? That explained the price - $500 a pound! I'd sooner wear one on my finger than eat it. Michel, the vendor, explained that truffles come in all sizes, from as small as a pea to as big as a cantaloupe, and can range in color from black to white.

"They can be hard or soft and taste like a nut or garlic. I have over twenty-five varieties of truffles on my property, the best are the black truffles of Perigord." Michel lowered his voice, "Don't be fooled by the inexpensive truffles exported to America. They are second-rate. Restaurants buy them for forty dollars a pound but they are not the real thing." He picked up a truffle and sliced it with his knife.

"You see how it is black inside and out? That is the sign of a good truffle. If it is black on the outside and yellow or white inside, it is no good."

It wasn't clear to me how you "farm" a fungus. Michel explained that truffles are found at the base of oak trees. "You plant an oak, wait and hope." It was a high risk crop with a big pay off. Michel's truffle farm was in Cahors in the Lot Department, about two-hundred miles northeast of where we were. Harvesting truffles, November through March, was done with the help of dogs or pigs who found the odor of truffles to be similar to that of the wild boar in heat. Talk about sex appeal! Imagine the first person who saw a pig, rooting around at the base of a tree, eating a black fungus and thought, "Oh, I want to taste *that*!"

Given the price, truffles are used sparingly, most often "shaved" on top of a slice of foie gras or an omelet. But Michel, who comes from a region that farms 200 tons of truffles a year, had a more indulgent suggestion.

"Eat them *whole* like a vegetable," he said.

He gave me a recipe for whole truffles baked in salt. At those prices, it wasn't going to happen in my kitchen but I could envision *Posh* readers salivating.

I met up with Sheila for late afternoon tea at a sidewalk café. We swapped stories about our purchases, or rather, her purchases and my "notes." Sheila's tote bag was weighted down with souvenir cans of foie gras.

"Gotta keep my departmental colleagues happy," she said.

Given Shelia's appetite, I wouldn't have been surprised if her tote bag was empty before she landed in Newark.

"Did you know they only use *male* ducks for foie gras?" she said, then went off on a tangent about gender, food and sex, three topics on which she had built her academic career and, from what I could gather, her personal life.

"Hey, look who it is," Sheila said, interrupting herself, as only a true monologue artist can.

"What? Where?"

"Over there, across the street."

I followed her gaze. It was Monsieur Picard with a willowy blond, his hand on her arm.

"I'll bet that's not his daughter," said Sheila.

"Maybe it's his sister."

"Yeh, and I'm Queen of Siam." Sheila had a wicked gleam in her eyes. "Well, there's one way to find out." She waved her napkin in the air and called out, "YOO HOO! Monsieur Picard!"

I wanted to dive under the table. Picard whirled around, saw Sheila and me, managed a tight smile, then speed walked away from us, taking his friend with him. I didn't see her face but from her high-stepping gait and platinum mane, I could've sworn it was Sandrine de Fondeville. Putting that together with the knowledge I gained eavesdropping on her wax job, I began to suspect that Picard and Sandrine were, as Sheila would say, an "item."

"Well, why not? He's married to an old prune," she said.

I wondered aloud what ever brought them together.

"Money," snapped Sheila.

"How do you know?"

"I asked."

"You *what*?"

"One day when I was waiting for a taxi, I asked Madame Picard how she met her husband. I always ask. You'd be surprised what I hear," said Sheila, breaking off a tiny piece of an elephant ear.

"Madame Picard said her husband married her for money?"

"Not in those words," Sheila said, pecking away at her pastry. "She said she was vacationing in Monte Carlo after her first husband died. You know, the bereft widow crying into her chips at the roulette table. She won and lost a great deal of money. Emile worked at the casino as a dealer and I got the impression he had a lucrative sideline keeping rich old ladies happy."

"Emile was a *gigolo*?" The word felt strange in my mouth, like something I had coughed up.

"That's how it sounds to me. She hired him to run the hotel and, somewhere along the way, the benefits included marriage."

"I don't know. Madame Picard doesn't look the type to hang out in Monte Carlo or to pick up a gigolo."

"We're *all* the type. Trust me," Sheila said, brushing pastry crumbs off her blouse.

I had to admit, Emile and Sandrine made a rather spectacular couple. But if they were lovers, could it have been Sandrine, and not Nicole, that I heard arguing with Picard my first night at the hotel?

"Earth to Fedora!" Sheila said, pulling me out of my reverie.

"Oh, sorry. I was just thinking about something that happened this morning."

I recounted my *faux pas* at the beauty salon causing Sheila to laugh in big gulps, tears streaming down her face. Our conversation meandered to from small talk to the personal, which happens with startling speed whenever two women of shared sensibilities discover one another, whether in an airport restroom or an outdoor café in southwest France. We dissected our marriages, the one to which I was still desperately clinging, and the two Sheila had happily left in her wake. I was energized by Sheila's positive, take-no-prisoner's outlook. So what if my marriage was over, Sheila reasoned? I was still young enough to experience *une grande amour*. So what if Paul was prickly?

"In three days, you'll never see him again," she said.

To celebrate my newfound sense of entitlement, I bought a ridiculously expensive peach charmeuse nightgown at a boutique in Eauze. Sheila bought a lavender lace bustier. We giggled all the way back to our hotel.

I went to my room, put on my new nightie and admired myself in the full length mirror of the armoire. Yes, indeedy. I was a Babe. Only one small detail. I twisted off my wedding ring and placed it in the nightstand drawer. I was awakened by a hand clamped over my mouth. I opened my eyes. It was Jacques.

Part II

The heart has its reasons of which reason knows nothing.
- Blaise Pascal

17

"Do not make a sound," he said. He reeked of alcohol, tobacco and garlic.

Something glinted in his other hand. It was a Laguiole knife. My scream was automatic. So was the hand that covered my mouth again.

"*Ecoutez-moi*," he whispered hoarsely. "I will not harm you. Be quiet. Do as I say."

I wagged my head in terrified agreement. But if this was rape, I would not be quiet or compliant. I'd yell my head off and poke his eyes out.

"Get up. Put your clothes on," he ordered.

I stood up, walked to the closet and eyed the door. This was my chance. No time for false modesty. I tore out of the room and ran down the stairs. I tripped and fell on the landing. He grabbed me, slapped a strip of adhesive over my mouth, tied my hands and feet like a calf and carried me, wriggling and wild-eyed, to a flatbed truck parked outside. No curious guests opened their doors to see what the commotion was about. No one was at the front desk. Not even the dogs.

"I *told* you to get dressed. It's cold," he said angrily, as if admonishing a child.

Cold? It was fucking freezing! He threw blankets over me that smelled like sheep, then he got into driver's seat and off we went to God knows where. I squirmed and twisted around to try to see where we were going. All I saw were a zillion stars. We were hundred of miles from any sizeable city. There were no earthly lights to compete with the dazzling show up above. I looked up into Van Gogh's *Starry Night* and calmed myself by identifying Orion and the Big Dipper.

There's nothing like being kidnapped to put your priorities into focus. It's faster and cheaper than analysis. Less time consuming than keeping a journal. And from the thumping inside my chest, I'd say it's one hell of a cardio workout. Ironically, as I bounced around on the back of the truck, I wasn't worried about what would happen to me. I worried about my family. My parents, my brothers and sisters. Even my cat. I never took their feelings into consideration when I quit my job at the *Daily Star* and accepted this travel writing gig.

It occurred to me that everything I do – everything *anyone* does - has a ripple effect, impacting the lives of everyone else. If I get out of this alive, I vowed, I will be more considerate of others. I won't cut my sisters off when they whine about their diets. I'll be nicer to my mother. Not that I'm mean, but you know how it is when you're over thirty-five and your Mom still picks lint off your clothes. And I'll upgrade my cat's food to gourmet kitty soufflés.

Bumping along on the cold, dark road, I thought about my marriage. "You should've given him children," said my grandmother. "You should've given him more home cooked meals," counseled my mother. "You should've given him a blow job," said my sister Ro. In retrospect, I had given Arthur two out of three on a fairly frequent basis. In Napoleon's France, young girls were groomed to be courtesans, instructed in the art of pleasing men. The only tip my mother gave me prior to my wedding night was, "Put it between two pieces of wax paper and pound it with a mallet." One can only hope she was talking about veal scaloppini.

I allowed myself to gloat momentarily at the image of Arthur rending his Armani suits upon hearing of my untimely death. I saw him thrashing about, wailing inconsolably, blaming himself for not being a faithful husband. Then I saw him pull himself together, go shopping for a new suit and book a cruise to Tahiti with his lover.

If I died, there'd be no divorce. No alimony. No tedious division of his assets. Arthur would be *thrilled*! Wait a sec. Maybe, just maybe, Arthur had arranged for me to "disappear" in France. No. He wouldn't. He couldn't. He's a lawyer.

But then I started thinking about murders I had investigated for the *Daily Star.* A highly respected Wilmington lawyer had disposed of an inconvenient girlfriend in a beer cooler off the Jersey shore. And there was the Cherry Hill rabbi who hired the Three Stooges to whack his wife because he feared that a divorce would tarnish his career.

Arthur was far more brilliant and cunning than either of those bozos. If anyone could pull off the perfect crime, he could. These were not rational thoughts but I was not in a rational situation. I was hog-tied, rolling around the back of a pickup truck, that, from what I could smell, was used to haul manure. With adrenaline fueling my brain, I focused on the first two things I would do if I survived this ordeal. Tell my mother I loved her and hire a divorce lawyer.

* * * *

The room was dark and reeked of garlic, not the kind that wafted from my grandmother's kitchen, but a pungent odor that stung my nostrils and made my eyes tear. Angry voices came from the other side of a door. I was still wearing that gossamer thin nightgown. The floor felt like ice under my bare feet. I knocked over something that made a loud metallic noise when it hit the floor. The voices stopped. The door opened and someone entered. A light went on, momentarily blinding me. My visitor was an old woman with a face like a rotten potato.

I looked up and saw the source of the stench, garlic garlands hung from the ceiling, hundreds of them, enough to ward off all the vampires in Europe. Mrs. Potato Head shoved a bundle of rags into my hands. With gestures and grunts, she helped me get dressed in a stiff shirt, a scratchy woolen skirt that barely came to my knees, thick socks and a large, black shawl. If there was a casting call for a dinner theater version of *Les Mis*, I was ready. She shuffled out and came back in the room with a steaming bowl of broth.

"*Mangez. Mangez.*" she ordered.

The soup was pink. I took a sip. If it was poison, it was well seasoned. The crone gave me a toothless smile and waddled out of the room. The door creaked open again. I recognized the barrel chest, the broken nose, the scar.

"*Ça va?*" said Jacques.

I backed away.

"Don't be afraid," he said, "I won't hurt you."

"Where am I?"

"Sit down," Jacques said softly. I sat, but at a distance on a wobbly wooden chair.

"The soup, it is good, *non*?" he asked, as if I had just stopped by for lunch.

"What is it?"

"*Ail rouge,* pink garlic soup," he said, "It only grows here in the Midi. You should come for the Garlic Festival in July."

Oh, sure, I'd love to wake up in Garlickville on a regular basis. Perhaps they have a Kidnap Festival.

"Where am I?" I repeated.

"My mother's house."

Jacques said we were just outside Lautrec, the birthplace of the artist, northwest of Toulouse. He took out his knife, opened it. I was about to scream but stopped as he cut down a garlic bulb, peeled it and popped it into his mouth as if it were a grape.

"I must leave France," he said, "I need money."

"I'm a journalist. Journalists don't have money. You want money? You should've kidnapped a lawyer."

"You are American. All Americans have money." he said and handed me a cell phone.

No way was I calling Arthur. My primary motivation for taking this job was to make him miss me. To admit I needed him was unthinkable.

"How much do you need?" I asked.

Jacques conferred with Mama.

"Fifty thousand."

"Euros or dollars?" I asked.

Mama shouted "Euros."

That was eighty grand. My parents did not have that kind of money; they were retired public school teachers, living on their modest pension. My brother and sisters? They were drowning in student loans, mortgages and daycare. The only person who might be able to come up with big bucks was Sissy. She answered on the second ring.

"Hiya, Doll!" said Sissy, "I'm at Ben & Irv's Deli. We were standin' in line for *hours*. You'll *never* guess who I met while waiting…"

Sissy, the Monologue Queen, didn't make conversation. She made pronouncements. Normally, I waited for her to run to the end of her loop. With Jacques breathing garlic fumes down my neck, I cut her off.

"Sissy," I said, "I'VE BEEN KIDNAPPED!"

There was a pause on the other end, then laughter.

"Fedora, if this is a joke, it is *not* funny," she said, "Sol, you gotta here this. Tell Sol."

Sol Spivak got on the phone.

"Babe, we're just sittin' down to eat," he said, "You ever had a Jewish hoagie at Ben and Irv's? Over a pound of corned beef, roast beef, salami, pastrami and Swiss cheese with the works."

I was not in the mood to ask in what Universe a sandwich of meat and dairy products could possibly be labeled "Jewish" or why Sol, who had so many bypass procedures he had his own parking space at Einstein Hospital, was about to eat one.

"This is serious!" I shouted, "People have been killed!"

Sol put Sissy back on the line.

"Ok. Just say yes or no. Is someone holding a gun to your head?"

I looked at Jacques' paring knife.

"Yes."

"Is he there right now?"

"Yes."

"Let me talk to him."

"I don't think that's a good idea."

"LEMME TALK TA HIM!" Sissy yelled.

I handed the phone to Jacques. He walked in circles, the phone pressed to his ear.

"Who is *thees* idiot?" he grumbled, handing the phone back to me.

"My boss."

"She is *dément!*"

"Sissy? It's me."

"Okay, hon. I got Frenchie down to one thou. I'll transfer the funds into your checking account after we stop off at Baskin Robbins. I'm on a new high fat diet," she said.

"How long is this going to take?" I asked.

"I dunno. A couple of months? My goal is to be a size six by New Year's Eve."

"No, Sissy. HOW LONG WILL IT TAKE FOR THE MONEY TO TRANSFER?"

"How should I know? It's a computer thingy. I really don't understand how you get yourself into these *situations*. When you get back, I want you to see my acupuncturist. She'll realign your chakras."

I didn't think so.

18

At the first light of dawn, Mama came in with a bowl of frothy café latté. Room service. Who knew? I wrapped a blanket around my shoulders and took the coffee outside. The doors were not locked. The next dwelling was miles away. If I wanted to make my getaway, what would I do, wave down a sheep?

The coffee warmed my hands and tasted yummy. The sky was moody, low gray clouds blocked out the sun. A peacock strutted across the yard, threading its way among the roving dogs, cats and hens. A horse poked his caramel face out of a faded red barn. It was more Currier and Ives than *In Cold Blood.* I was no longer frightened but eager to get back to the comforts of Chateau Mignon. I had slept in the clothes Mama had provided and felt as musty as an old mattress. Jacques started up his truck, a battered pickup that belched out black smoke.

"*Allons.* Get in," he called out of the window.

I climbed in the passenger seat and turned to look at the flatbed in the back, a rusted metal floor half-covered with an oily tarp. I remembered being bounced about on a cold, hard surface, the smell of diesel and the rumbling of tires. Jacques promised to take me to a place where I could get a taxi back to my hotel after he got his money. Fortuitously, every town in the Midi had a decent brasserie and an ATM. The one in Lautrec spat out crispy Euros, the equivalent of one thousand U.S. dollars. I gave Jacques the money.

"I did not kill Nicole," he said in a gravelly whisper.

"Then why are you running away?"

Jacques wiped his mouth with the back of his hand.

"When I was young, I went to prison for something I did not do. I will not go back. *Jamais*! I will go to California."

He showed me a crumpled, stained business card from a Sonoma vineyard that he had carried for so long it was almost illegible.

"The owner wants to produce Armagnac in California. He told me to call him when I'm ready."

An arson and murder suspect would not get through U.S. Customs.

"You need to clear yourself before going anywhere," I urged.

Jacques shook his head.

"I never touched Nicole. But they will blame me for her death."

"And the fire?" I asked.

"What   fire?

"At Chateau des Reves."

Jacques grabbed my shoulders and shook me.

"*My* vineyard? *My* grapes? When did this happen?"

"Saturday night, Sunday morning. You were there."

"No, I wasn't. I was…I was…"

"You came into the barn at Chateau des Reves around ten o'clock. You were drunk."

"*Non, non, non….*"

"You were shouting, fighting."

"Saturday night I went to a bar in the village. People saw me. They will remember. Maybe I drank too much."

"You pulled a knife on the Baron and his guests."

"I remember *nothing*," he cried. He crumbled down to the pavement, his head in his hands, rocking back and forth, sobbing. "My grapes. My grapes."

If he was acting, this was an Academy Award performance.

A taxi pulled up. I waved it away.

* * * *

"From the time Nicole arrived in the village, she hardly spoke a word to me. Just *bonjour, bonsoir, au revoir*. Then, one night, I come back to my cottage and there she was, waiting for me. I am not a fool, Mademoiselle. Nicole did not come to me for love. She came for protection."

"Protection from what?"

"I suppose it doesn't matter now," he sighed, "Nicole was *enceinte*."

"She was *what*?"

"*Enceinte.*" Jacques patted his stomach. Nicole was pregnant. "She had no family, nowhere to go, so she came to me. I asked nothing in return. We slept in separate beds. It sounds crazy, no?"

"Did you know who the father was?"

Jacques rubbed his scar as if it was a fresh wound.

"All I can tell you is what Nicole told me. The man could not marry her because he had a wife, a wife with a lot of money."

A married man with a rich wife? That described Picard, Fondeville and perhaps every vineyard owner in the Midi. A light rain started to fall. We ducked into a brasserie. It had a red awning imprinted with bright yellow letters: *Cafe de Paris*. Workmen stood at the bar throwing back shots of whisky for breakfast, businessmen sat at tables, dunking croissants in coffee. A few heads turned our way. We must've made quite a pair, Jacques with his frozen face, me dressed like a serf. Jacques went to the bar and brought back an espresso and whiskey for himself, a *café latte* and an almond croissant for me.

"Running away won't clear your name. It will make things worse. Come with me back to Mignon. Talk to Inspector Beaumonde. He will listen to you. He's a good man."

Jacques knocked back his whiskey in one gulp.

"A good man? One good man already sent me to prison. No, I won't do it."

"Then let me help you."

"What can you do?" he snorted.

Jacques was getting louder. The man at the next table expressed his indignation by refolding his newspaper with a flourish.

"I was an investigative reporter. If Nicole had enemies, give me their names. At least tell me the names of the men she was seeing. The sooner the person responsible is arrested, the sooner you can go back to your vineyard."

"You don't understand," he sighed. "I will never be able to go back if I betray my employer."

"Baron de Fondeville?"

"The baron is a *bon vivant.* He likes games of chance, roulette, baccarat and pretty girls. Nicole was one of many."

"Could he be the father of her child?"

Jacques stared out the window at gray sheets of rain falling on outdoor tables and chairs. The side of his face I could see was made of stone.

19

My hotel room at Chateau Mignon looked exactly as I had left it. Fresh sunflowers in the blue vase by the window. Foil-wrapped chocolates on starched pillows. Lavender soaps in the bathroom. Everything was in its place, except Paul. He had checked out of the hotel. I picked up the phone to call him, then put it down. I needed to build up my own ego before massaging his.

I stripped off the sackcloth garments, threw them in the waste basket and took a long, hot shower, double shampooing my hair to get rid of the *eau de garlic*. A quick towel dry and a shake of my head proved Antoinette's artistry was still intact. I changed into Levi's and an over-sized, gray cashmere sweatshirt which I had given Arthur for his fortieth birthday and subsequently re-gifted to myself.

Sitting cross-legged in bed, I checked my email. There were messages from Sissy, my mother and Detective Paramour. Sissy's messages were all in shout mode. ARE YOU OK? DID YOU GET THE $$$$? My mother forwarded a magazine article, *What Men Really Want,* written by a talk-radio psychologist who advocated Kegel exercises. The date was set for trial of Pee Wee, my adolescent assailant. It was in three weeks and I prayed it would be continuously delayed, like so many Philly court cases, until I was safely ensconced in a nursing home.

I rinsed out my nightie. I couldn't throw the filmy bit of indulgence away but I knew I would never wear it again without thinking of garlic. Having grown up in a home where everything happened in two realms, the Earthly and the Occult, I saw cause and effect where others just saw coincidence. I had removed my ring. Cause. I had been kidnapped: Effect. Ergo: The sooner I put my wedding ring back on my hand, the faster the Wheel of Karma will spin my way. I opened the drawer. There was nothing inside but a Bible.

* * * *

"We are not responsible for valuables. There is a safe in your room for that purpose," Monsieur Picard said.

"But it's my wedding ring."

"Then you should not have taken it off."

Something pressed on my sternum making it difficult to catch my breath. It was guilt.

"Listen, I am here as a travel writer to promote your hotel. If this is the kind of place where valuable jewelry disappears…"

"Madame Wolf," he said, slipping into a well-oiled managerial tone, "Ours is a small hotel with a staff that is like family. There is just my wife and myself, one chambermaid, a cook and a gardener. I will speak to them. Nothing is more important than the comfort and safety of our guests."

I had had this conversation before, but not with Picard. I was talking to Sheila. Something about missing jewelry, but what was it? I was trained to be good listener, but I'm often too busy listening to the fascinating conversation inside my own head.

* * * *

The best way to offset one anxiety is to focus on another. I returned to my room and composed a carefully worded email to Paul. The truth, that I was kidnapped and held for ransom, wouldn't fly. Instead, I appealed to his ego and his bank account. "My editor loves your photos. She wants to see more images of vineyard operations. Fedora."

It wasn't a lie as much as an embroidery of the truth. I hadn't sent Sissy any photos. If she really needed more images, I could get them from the Tourism Office. They could also provide me with another driver. That isn't what I wanted. I wanted Paul with his joke of a car, Gauloise and citrus aftershave. The guy smelled good and, if you have to travel with someone 24/7, that is no small factor.

And then there was my promise to Jacques to find Nicole's killer, or at least eliminate Jacques as a person of interest. I decided to start with Guy de Fondeville. He had access, means and motivation. The fire at his chateau might've been a decoy. Fondeville may have wanted to shift the attention away from Nicole's death and the fire simply got out of hand.

Setting up a meeting with the Baron didn't tax my creativity. All I had to do was pick up the phone, say my name, and let his imagination fill in the blanks.

20

"Where are you?" he said.

"At my hotel."

"What about your friend?"

"Paul? He went back to Toulouse."

Fondeville was using a flat tone of voice. Anyone listening on the other side would've thought he was speaking to a business associate.

"I'll be there in fifteen minutes."

I tucked my mini tape recorder into my bra, then waited in the lobby.

"Well, *there* you are!"

I'd know that voice anywhere. Sheila plunked herself down in the chair next to mine. She shot a glance at the reception desk where Picard was sorting mail and lowered her voice to a throaty whisper.

"It's getting kind of interesting around here," she said. "You know that Nicole woman they found in the field? She was a drug addict."

I raised my eyebrows which is all the encouragement Sheila needed.

"It conforms with my research on the subjection of women. Did you read my book? It isn't my best work, but you know how it is. Sex sells."

Sheila sputtered on and on until Fondeville sauntered in, all six foot-two of him, in a buff suede hunting jacket with a paisley ascot fluttering about his neck. When introduced to Sheila, he bowed gallantly and brought her plump hand to his lips. For once, Sheila was speechless.

* * * *

Guy de Fondeville held open the door of his silver Jaguar coupe. It was a sleek, low-slung model with a burled walnut dashboard and buttery leather seats. A far cry from Paul's 2CV.

"Isn't it a bit chilly to have the top down?" I asked.

"I'll turn the heat on and you can put this on your lap."

Fondeville reached behind the bucket seats and handed me a fur throw. There was nothing faux about it. It was black Russian sable. The Jaguar ate up the road, chewing the curves and spitting them out. Fondeville drove with one hand on the wheel, the other on the gear shift and, at times, my knee. *Vroom! Vroom!*

"I want you to feel something," he said. "Put your hand here."

Fondeville grabbed my left hand and placed it on the wheel.

"You're holding the reins on 300 horses," he shouted over the engine.

"I, I can't steer from here."

"Let me show you what it can do," he said.

Fondeville floored it, going ninety, a hundred miles per hour. I closed my eyes and cowered under the sable wrap, hoping my lack of enthusiasm would slow him down. It didn't. Our private Grand Prix ended in Vic-Fezensac, a town I had passed the day I landed in Toulouse.

* * * *

We entered a bar on the first floor of *La Vieille Ferme*, a small hotel. The tables were made of wine barrels, the burnt orange walls were covered with old bullfight posters.

"Bullfighting? In France?" I asked.

"*Bien sûr.* When I was a child, there were eight bullrings in the Midi. The biggest was *Soleil d'Or* in Toulouse. It held twelve thousand people. Here in Vic-Fezensac, there is an annual *feria*, a bullfighting festival. Thousands of people fill the streets, singing, dancing, drinking. No one sleeps for three days. It's *fantastique*."

"Bullfighting is inhumane. I don't like to see animals tortured."

"At least in France, the bull does not die. More often than not, it's the bullfighter that gets the worst of it," he said, reaching for my thigh under the table and giving it a squeeze.

I shifted my chair, angling it away from his reach. If the fire at his chateau was a tragedy, Fondeville masked it well. Nothing in his manner hinted at financial loss or personal despair. Still, I felt an expression of empathy was in order.

"I'm so sorry about the fire. This must be a very difficult time for you."

"Ah, well, you have to play the hand you are dealt," he mumbled into his brandy.

He drained his glass and swiveled, trying to catch the bartender.

"Would your wife be upset if she knew you were with me?"

"Fedora, you come from a country whose government came to a stop just because your president had sex with another woman. We French know what men do. We know what women do. Now tell me, *ma chère*, how about a *pousse rapier?*"

I hesitated. Was this some kinky sex thing?

Fondeville snapped his fingers and two glasses of bubbly arrived, each glass was decorated with a gilt sword.

"*Pousse-rapier* means sword thrust," Fondeville explained. "It's our most famous Gascon cocktail. You see the sword on the side of your glass? You pour Armagnac up to the bottom of the sword, then fill it up to the hilt with Brut de Monluc sparkling wine or Champagne."

Fondeville clicked his glass against mine. The cocktail was as light as a wine spritzer but with the sweet flavors of citrus and brandy. When I emptied my glass, he snapped his fingers again. Two drinks before lunch? Time wasn't just standing still, it was going sideways.

A terrine of *foie gras* and toast points appeared. Anyone who has attended a wine tasting, whether in France or New Jersey, has received a lecture on pairing, the importance of matching wines to the appropriate food. I always found such talk pretentious and got a kick out of ordering the least expensive red wine on the menu, no matter what I was eating. That is, until my *pousse-rapier* met the subtle flavor of the *foie gras*. They didn't just pair, they fell into each other's arms and eloped. I felt emboldened.

"How did you meet Sandrine?"

"Why do you ask?"

"Because I want to know *everything* about you."

In my line of work, I find that once you get someone talking about themselves they rarely run out of things to say. Fondeville studied my face, his eyes drifted lower as if assessing the fair trade value of his disclosure.

"We met at an engagement party. I had seen Sandrine's photograph in magazines but, in person, she was...she was *sensationnel.* I had to have her."

"Was it mutual?"

"Yes, but there were complications. You see, the party was in honor of Sandrine's engagement to my cousin."

"What happened?"

Fondeville poured himself another glass of champagne.

"Sandrine married me. My cousin married another blonde."

"Why do you think she chose you?"

"I had a faster car and a, uh, larger… château. Marrying a Baron impressed Sandrine's fashion friends in Paris but I sometimes wonder…"

He stared into his glass.

"What?" I prodded.

"When we met, Sandrine was at the peak of her modeling career, running off to Gstadd and Cap de Ferrat with *Le Comte de* this and *Le Duc de* that. Life in the Midi can be dull for a woman of her temperament. She's always finding excuses to run to Paris, these endless shopping trips. How many pairs of shoes does a woman need?"

Fondeville's ironic tone seemed a flimsy bandage over a deeper wound. Sandrine, the Great Beauty he had won away from his cousin, had grown bored, restless. Was insecurity the engine that drove him from one unmade bed to the next? Or was Fondeville merely an aging skirt chaser, using his wife's imaginary infidelities to justify his own philandering?

"I heard about you and Nicole," I said, moving closer to him so as to better position my tape recorder. Fondeville addressed himself attentively to my décolleté.

"Is that so?" His tone was light, as if I had commented on the weather.

"Is it true you were lovers?"

"It was purely physical. Nicole had a raw, animal quality."

Fondeville lit up a cigar.

"Try this," he said, holding the moistened tip to my lips.

Sometimes a cigar is just a cigar. Not *this* time.

21

As any married woman knows, beds and sex are not necessarily synonymous. That's what I told myself as Fondeville steered me up a flight of stairs into a room above the bar for "dessert." I was determined to hold onto my panties and dignity even though my blood alcohol content was just this side of embalmed. I reminded myself, this is why they call it "undercover" work.

Fondeville disappeared into the bathroom. I pulled the tape recorder out of my bra, wrapped it up in my scarf and arranged it on the table next to the bed. That way, if he got me into a clinch, he wouldn't know I was wired.

The bathroom door opened. Baron Guy de Fondeville emerged looking like the star of *La Cage Aux Folles* in black lace panties, a filmy black peignoir, his eyes smoldered with kohl, his cheeks were rouged and his lips glistened with lipstick, the same deep plum shade Nicole had worn. The Baron had nice body work for his age, washboard abs, a natural blond from what I could see, but I had to bite my cheek to keep from laughing.

Is this why Sandrine was always running to Paris? I blinked back images of my Arthur prancing about in lingerie. No. Impossible. But maybe. Guy de Fondeville strutted around the room like a super model, then arranged himself seductively on the bed.

"Well?" he asked.

"That lipstick's a good shade for you," I said diplomatically.

I was being polite. He would've looked better in a peachy coral.

"Fedora, are you going to join me or do you prefer to *watch*?"

"Well, actually, I've never ….."

"NEVER?" Guy's eyes bulged comically.

"I mean…not with a *married* man."

"*Vive la différence, chérie,*" he sighed.

Guy slid under the sheets, wriggled out of his (or her) panties and beckoned for me to join him. There is nothing quite so ridiculous as being fully dressed in the presence of a naked man wearing lipstick. I slipped off my shoes and perched on the far side of the bed.

"How did Nicole come to work at the Château?"

"I don't want to talk about Nicole. It's *you* who's driving me mad," he said taking my foot in his hand.

"Well, I'm interested in what attracted a man of your stature to a…."

"To a *putain?*"

"Well, yes."

"All men desire mindless whores. If I want intellectual companionship, I have my wife… or someone else's."

"If Nicole was so 'mindless', why did you hire her to work in the gift shop?"

"Hiring Nicole was Sandrine's idea. I was against it. Her image was all wrong for our clientele. Sandrine insisted. It was a disaster."

"In what way?"

Fondeville nibbled on my toes. The sensation was, um, stimulating.

"You can put a chimpanzee in a Dior gown, but it will still swing from the trees," he said.

He drew my big toe into his warm, wet mouth. I felt a tremor along my inner thigh. If I wasn't careful, the only incriminating evidence I would get on this tape would be my own.

"Did you know Nicole was pregnant?" I asked.

Fondeville stopped sucking my toes. His magic sword shrank back inside its sheath.

"Do you want to fuck or do you want to talk?"

His tone was polite as if he were asking me if I wanted red wine or white.

"I'm sorry," I stammered. "I find you very attractive but…but I'm married."

Fondeville's lips curled into a lopsided smile as if I had just said something hilarious.

"And so am I, my dear. But all this chatter gives me a headache. I find a good, strong fuck to be excellent for the circulation. And, if I do say so, you look as if you could use one."

"I'll be right back," I said and scurried to the bathroom. I splashing cold water my face, then I played around with the bidet. Never could figure them out. Then I tried on the miniature hand creams and moisturizers. When I came out, Guy was splayed across the bed, eyes closed. Letting him sleep it off seemed a better idea that waking him. I carefully stretched out on the opposite side of the bed, fully clothed, and placed two pillows vertically between us as a barrier. Moments later, I heard snoring of an assuredly aristocratic mode.

22

"Bonjour," chirped a voice on the phone, "Will you be staying with us another day?"

"Whaaa? Wha time izzit?"

"It is eleven a.m., mademoiselle. Check out time."

I had slept like a rock, a rock at the bottom of an armagnac sea. I turned my head, slowly and painfully. A bouquet of golden curls bloomed on the adjacent pillow.

"*Merci,*" I said, "We will vacate the room *toute suite.*"

To his credit, Guy had not taken advantage of the situation. He had remained as still as a fallen soldier on his side of the bed the entire night and half the next day.

"Guy?" I said gently nudging his shoulder. He didn't budge. I yanked back the covers. He didn't stir. I couldn't help noticing that his sword was drawn and thrusting. I cranked up the volume.

"GUY! WAKE UP!

I have been told that I have a voice that can wake the dead. Not this time. Baron de Fondeville had checked out for good. Gathering up my things and taking a cab back to my hotel was not an option. Too many people had seen us: Sheila, probably Picard, the waiter in the hotel bar, certainly the concierge who gave Fondeville a room key and saw us climb the stairs together. I called down to the front desk and explained the situation. At first, the concierge misunderstood and wanted to send for a doctor.

"It's too late," I said, "He is dead."

I asked him to call the police.

Wanting to see for himself, the concierge raced to the room, took one terrified look at Fondeville, crossed himself and went flying out again.

* * * *

Inspector Beaumonde stared at me so intently that my right eyelid start to flicker. It does that when I'm nervous.

"You pulled the sheets down like this?" he asked.

"Yes."

"And you did not move him or change anything?"

"No."

Before calling the concierge, I had removed all traces of cosmetics from the Baron's face with a warm washcloth. I hid his panties and peignoir in my bag, a small gesture to preserve the dignity of a man who had precious little left.

"No one else entered the room after you retired last night?"

"I don't think so but I can't be sure. I had quite a bit to drink."

"And   monsieur?

"We both had armagnac cocktails and wine."

The Inspector's tone was flat, the monotone of criminal investigation. His eye's scanned Guy's body as if the clue to his death was lying on display. He seemed to pay special attention to the Baron's penis which was still pointing toward Toulouse.

"Tell me again. When did you and Monsieur de Fondeville first become *intime*?

"Ah, well, we didn't. That is, he fell asleep while I was in the bathroom."

"He fell asleep *before* sex?" he asked, his voice and his eyebrows arching to new heights.

"There was no sex," I whined.

I was exhausted, dehydrated, hungry. Would it be *gauche* to ask for a continental breakfast in the presence of a dead body? The Inspector looked inside the bathroom.

"Yours?" He asked, returning into the room with a small black vinyl zippered case with the Dior logo. The Baron's cosmetic bag!

"Oh, yes, thank you."

"And this?" He said, pointing to an object on the nightstand.

Oh, Jesus. My tape recorder. Beaumonde hit reverse, then play. Guy's voice filled the room. *Give me your hand. I want you to feel something. Feel that Fedora? That's 300 horses.*

Beaumonde pinched the skin between his brows and closed his eyes. When he opened them, his pupils had the accusatory stare of a dead mackerel.

23

When a sexually adventurous woman dies before her time, the call for justice is drowned out by mean-spirited slander. She was a whore, she *deserved* it. But when a philandering *bon vivant* bites the dust, he is elevated to sainthood before the coffin is lowered.

In every bar in Gascony, men raised a glass to the Baron. Women wept copiously, causing their husbands to silently wonder about the paternity of their children. Members of the *Compagnie des Mousquetaires*, attended the Baron's wake, capes flapping like giant pigeons. They provided a horse-drawn carriage for his funeral procession. I learned all of this from Madame Picard who gave a detailed account of the events, right down to the cut of the Sandrine's mourning clothes.

"La Baroness wore vintage Chanel. *Trés apropos*. And the Baron, so handsome a man, was laid to rest with his sword and cape. In the eulogy, his comrades called the Baron 'the last of the Musketeers.'" She paused to wipe a tear. "This is the end of an era, *Mademoiselle*. There will never be another like him."

I couldn't have agreed more. I did not volunteer that I was the last one to see the Baron alive, when he was wearing an even more exciting costume. I hoped to be long gone before my presence at the Baron's deathbed became known, not just to Madame Picard but, more importantly, to Paul. With only three days before I was to leave France, I wanted to find a way to reconcile with him. But how? I thought back to when I first had problems in my marriage.

"Ah, *mi dios!*" my grandmother Gabriella cried, pointing to the seemingly random formation of sea shells she had thrown on the dining room table. She used the shells to communicate with her Santeria spirits. (I'm Cuban on my mother's side. Hungarian on my father's. The combination is responsible for frequent indigestion.) Gabriella scared me. Ever since I was a toddler, she could tell what I was thinking. She knew instantly which of us kids had squirted bubble bath into the washing machine, used her nail polish on the dog or buried one of her miniature saints in the sandbox.

"There is distance between you and Arthur," she said. "He is being drawn to another. It is a very strong sexual attraction. Here is what you do, Fedorita. Write Arthur's name on a piece of brown paper and place it in a large jar together with a piece of his clothing. A sock or something. Then fill the jar with orange blossom water, honey and a little of your pee pee. You must then spit in the jar three times, close it tightly, wrap it in a used pair of your underpants and hide it in the back of your closet. Every time Arthur becomes cold or indifferent, go into the closet and shake the jar."

"I am not going to keep a jar of urine in the closet." I said emphatically.

"Would you rather sleep alone?"

Begrudgingly, Gabriella relented and suggested a spell not involving bodily fluids. All I had to do was write Arthur's name vertically and horizontally on a piece of paper so that it formed a cross.

"It will not work as well but it is better than nothing," she sighed, gathering up her conch shells.

I never followed up on her advice. What I wanted from my grandmother, and always got, was her unconditional love, endless cups of tea and thick slices of homemade coconut cake, slathered with butter cream icing. I was a journalist; I put my faith in rigorous analysis of facts, not supernatural incantations. And yet, I wondered. What if Gabriella's spells were about *intention*, focusing the mind on a desired outcome? Even the Dali Lama and Bill Gates subscribed to that. Feeling as silly as a teenager carving initials into a tree, I wrote Paul's name horizontally and vertically on hotel stationary, then pierced it with a safety pin. I had nothing to lose.

24

Someone knocked lightly on the door. Paul? It was the chambermaid, a mousey teenager with an armful of clean towels. Her name was Josie and her English was good enough. I engaged her in conversation while she went about her chores.

"Last summer, I work for a family in London," she said. "Someday, I work in *Yoo Ess*. I go to Hollywood."

For girls like Josie, Hollywood was a place where chambermaids and prostitutes with no discernable talent could make it Big.

"Here's my card," I said, "If you come to the States, let me know. I have friends in Los Angeles."

I had worked in the film biz as a "reader" for one whiplash year between college and working at the *Daily Star*. Readers are people, typically English majors in their early twenties, who do what Hollywood agents and producers are loathe to do; they read. They read screenplays and write something called "coverage," a two-page synopsis which can yank a screenwriter from obscurity or bury him alive. I quickly soured on reading what seemed to be the same story over and over – talented, ambitious Everyman (or woman) overcomes impossible odds (poverty, illness, sexual orientation, bad hair, etc) to achieve their Big Dream (love, babies, expensive shoes).

I also tired of writing in the frosty second person which coverage required. "We lose interest in the hero after he shoots the dog and sets his girlfriend's hair on fire." Frankly, after a year of reporting to middle-aged men with pony tails, *we* couldn't wait to get back East and sink our teeth into a real job and a Philly cheese steak.

Josie looked at my card as if it was a winning lottery ticket. I didn't bother to explain that my LA friends were mostly failed actors and writers who walked other people's dogs, parked their cars and served them double decaf lattes.

"*Merci, Madame.* You are so kind."

I wasn't kind. I was calculating. Maids are the invisible cameras of any hotel. They see what management would prefer to keep hidden. I opened a drawer and offered Josie my secret stash of Double Chocolate Milanos. Who brings baked goods to France? I do.

Josie slipped a cookie into her pocket and set about cleaning the bathroom. I stood in the doorway, nibbling on a Milano, careful not to get crumbs on the tiled floor. Visions of my Hollywood connections got Josie in a chatty mood.

"Were you friends with Nicole?" I asked.

"Friends? No. Nicole was, how you say…?" Josie flicked the tip of her nose with her finger.

"A snob?"

"*Oooh la la.* She was too good for me. Too good for this place."

"Did she talk about her family?"

"Sometimes. She say her mother is very, very rich. Then she say her mother is dead. With Nicole, you never know."

"Did Nicole have a boyfriend?"

"Didi. She stole him from me. She didn't really want him. You know what I mean?"

I wagged my head in agreement. I knew exactly what Josie meant. I had a friend in college who couldn't resist trying on other people's boyfriends just for size. Josie was bristling with hurt and jealousy. But was that enough to murder her rival?

"What's this Didi look like?"

"He has curly, dark hair and wears a black leather jacket and pants with lots of zippers."

She gave me everything but his inseam. If this character was still lurking around, he wouldn't be hard to miss.

"Now that Nicole is gone, will you and Didi…?"

She shook her head vigorously before I could finish.

"Never."

Methinks the lady protests too much. Besides, at her age, "never" lasts about fifteen minutes.

"Why not?" I prodded.

"When Didi was with me, he was a good guy. Nicole changed him."

"How?"

"*Drogues.*"

For a moment, I didn't understand. Then it sank in. Drugs.

"Is that why Nicole was fired?"

Josie smoothed her uniform, a gray smock, several sizes too large for her, that buttoned up the front and had two large pockets. She could have been a matron in a women's prison.

"She was fired because she was a thief."

"How do you know?"

"Things were missing from guest's rooms. Who else could it be? She and I were the only ones who had keys beside Madame and Monsieur Picard."

There was a knock at the door. Again, I thought Paul. Again, I was disappointed. It was Sheila, flushed and breathless from climbing the stairs. Josie grabbed up a pile of dirty towels and scurried out the door.

"This is like climbing the fucking Matterhorn," she sighed. "Am I interrupting?"

Without waiting a beat, she plopped herself down on my bed.

"I thought you were in the room next to mine on the first floor?" she said.

"That was my colleague's room. He's gone now."

"Oh, good. Then you're coming with me to Lourdes."

25

Lourdes is the punch line of a joke. In *Annie Hall*, Woody Allen tells Diane Keaton that he's been in analysis for 15 years. "I'm going to give it one more year, then I'm going to Lourdes," he says. Or something like that. So when Sheila Schlossberg-Koon suggested I accompany her to Lourdes, I couldn't help myself. I burst out laughing.

"No. Really," she said. "It's just an hour or two away. How can you be so close and not go?"

"Sheila, I don't believe in miracles and the thought of all those people throwing off their crutches, well, it's creepy."

"Of course, it's creepy. It's mass hysteria. That's exactly why you should go. Not because you believe in it, but because it's part of the history, the *culture* of southwest France. If you're in Rome, you go to the Vatican, right? In Jerusalem, you go to the Wall. You're in the Midi Pyrenees? You go to Lourdes."

Actually, I didn't have to go anywhere. I could've spent the entire day in my room banging out my article for *Posh* and waiting to hear from Paul. But seeing two dead bodies in one week and being kidnapped had me jumping at shadows. Which is why I went to Lourdes with Sheila. My number one bad habit, according to my second grade teacher Mrs. Zipperman, was impulsivity. Do, then think.

* * * *

"Your first visit to Lourdes?" asked our driver, a middle-aged man in a Basque beret who had the disconcerting habit of making eye contact with us in the rear view mirror. Look at the road, I wanted to scream.

"*Wee wee*," said Sheila.

"I take many people there, mostly British," he said. "Where you from?"

"New York," said Sheila.

The road, I thought. Look at the fucking road or we'll all be on crutches *before* we get to Lourdes.

"Don't encourage him," I whispered to Sheila. "Let him drive."

"Will you ree-lax?" she said, patting my thigh as if calming a testy toddler.

Usually, when anyone orders me to relax, I do the opposite and explode like a Chinese firecracker. Not with Sheila. Her steamroller persona and Rubenesque (make that Bottero) physique made me feel safe. No one would ever kidnap Sheila Schlossberg-Koon. And no harm would come to me, I reasoned, while I was with her. It was all I could do to resist climbing into her well-upholstered lap and suck my thumb.

"Five million people go to Lourdes every year," our driver said. "Most of them old and sick. Or young and sick. It's very sad."

Turn the car around, I thought. I hate crowds. I'm not too fond of hospitals. I catch colds easily.

"Sheila, maybe this isn't such a good idea. Five million *sick* people?" I said.

"They're not all going to be there at one time," she said. "And anyway, I'm sure they're not contagious."

Sure? How can anyone be sure these days? Legionnaires Disease! Swine flu! Anthrax!

"No," said the drive. "Today, you see only a few thousand."

Swell.

* * * *

We took N21 south, a decent four-lane road where cars could pass without saying the rosary. After a small town named Rabastens de Bigorre, our driver informed us we were no longer in the Gers *department.* We were in Hautes Pyrenées, heading straight toward the mountains in the distance. Lourdes was only another twenty minutes.

"If you like, we stop in Tarbes. You go to café, get something to eat or drink," said our driver, indicating that this is what sensible tourists do and, more importantly, this is what he wanted to do. My bladder thought it was an excellent idea.

I expected Tarbes to be one more small village, blink and it's gone. As it turned out, it was the second largest city in the Midi, next to Toulouse. Our driver parked in front of a brasserie. He headed for the bar, where working men stood, eating and drinking the same fare served at considerably higher prices in the dining room where we sat. Sheila and I ordered Quiche Lorraine and salads. She had cappuccino. I had tea. Any more coffee and I'd be twitching like a squirrel on crack.

"Do you know the Lourdes story?" Sheila asked.

"Wasn't it a movie?"

"*The Song of Bernadette,* 1943, starring Jennifer Jones. I must've seen it a dozen times on late night TV. Soppy movie but it leaves you wondering."

"Wondering what?"

"Whether the Virgin Mary really appeared to a fourteen-year-old French farm girl. The thing is, it happened in 1858. Who knew from psychosis then? Or brain tumors? Supposedly, this kid, Bernadette, is out collecting wood with two friends. They decide it's time to go home but she heads deeper into the woods. They tell her not to go there, just like in a horror film. *DON'T GO!* "

"Of course, Jennifer Jones, I mean Bernadette, keeps going. She sees a mysterious light that guides her to a grotto. There's no water in the grotto. But the Virgin Mary appears and tells Bernadette to *bathe* there. Interestingly, both Hollywood and the Catholic Church have this kid seeing the Virgin Mary, but in real life she claimed to have seen a beautiful *child* her own age. Aren't you going to finish that?"

I had left half my quiche and salad on the plate. When I'm nervous, I can't eat. And I was plenty nervous, wondering what vision of human suffering lay in wait for us at Lourdes. Sheila happily reached for my plate and rambled on.

"There's no water but the vision told her to bathe, so Bernadette comes back and digs until she finds water. Holy water, right? Her parent, meanwhile, don't believe her. The clergy aren't too thrilled either. Think about it. A fourteen-year-old girl comes home late, after dark, soaking wet with leaves in her hair. What parent is going to buy a story about an apparition in the woods? No, they're gonna smack her six ways to Sunday until she tells them the name of the guy who put that look of ecstasy on her face."

"Now here's where it gets interesting. They put Bernadette on *trial*. Vincent Price played the prosecutor. Jennifer Jones sticks to her guns. Instead of burning her at the stake, she goes into a convent where she gets cancer and dies. She's lying there, writhing in agony - young and beautiful and in horrible pain – and the Virgin Mary appears to Bernadette. For this, Jennifer Jones wins an Academy Award and we get a Saint." Sheila paused for that to sink in and, like the college professor she was, she rambled on as if lecturing in an ampitheater.

"Here's what I don't get. If Bernadette was on speaking terms with the Mother of God and had access to the miraculous healing waters of the grotto, why the fuck wasn't she *healed*?" Waving her fork, Sheila answered her own question. "Here's what I think happened. The cancer was probably in her *head* when she first saw lights and hallucinations. My uncle had cancer and when it got to his brain his entire personality changed. He went from being a pussy cat to a son of a bitch."

"Did he see the Virgin Mary?" I asked.

"No. He saw his lawyer and cut everyone out of his will."

* * * *

The Pyrenees Mountains danced before us like a mirage. The closer we got, the further away they shrank from our reach. They were magnificent. Rugged purple peaks with snowy caps jutting up into a cobalt sky. On the other side, Spain.

"Wow! Will you look at *that*." said Sheila.

In the shadow of the towering mountains there was a small, inconsequential, little village that would be no more than a pit stop for skiers and climbers, if it wasn't for the visions of a fourteen-year-old girl.

"You know how many hotels there are in Lourdes?" Asked our driver.

We didn't.

"Two hundred and seventy. More than any city in France, except Paris."

As we drove into the center of the village, my worst fears were confirmed. Everywhere I looked, there were shops selling tacky religious memorabilia. How tacky? Imagine enough Virgin Mary magnets to cover every refrigerator in the world. People did not move with the purposeful gait of pedestrians going to and from home, shopping or business. They moved like colonies of ants, invading one tourist trap, then the next.

"I drop you here and pick you up in four hours," our driver said, leaving us in front of a Best Western Hotel.

Four hours? I didn't think I could take it.

"C'mon," said Sheila, guidebook in one hand. "First, we go to the Basilica. They hold mass in twenty-five languages, twenty-four hours a day."

"Oh, I don't know. I haven't been to mass since.."

Since my grandfather's funeral. I was fifteen and so upset by my grandmother's heart-wrenching sobs that I didn't take it all in. I just remember a lot of flowers, candles and Kleenex.

"Sheila, are you Catholic?" I asked.

"God no. I'm an atheist. My interest in Lourdes is strictly academic. Richard Dawkin, the British evolutionary biologist, came here to research his book *Root of All Evil.* He found that every one of the sixty-seven 'miraculous healings' recognized by the Catholic Church were diseases that commonly go into remission. These people weren't permanently healed, their illnesses came back. Not one of them experienced a real miracle, like the reappearance of a severed limb."

"So, if you don't believe any of this, why is it so important to be here?"

"Because *they* believe," Sheila said, waving her arm toward hundreds, perhaps thousands of people moving, ever so slowly, toward the Basilica.

They represented every nationality, speaking a veritable Babel of languages: Chinese, Spanish, Portuguese, Russian, Italian, Japanese. Some were being pushed in wheelchairs and even beds, others zooming along in motorized carts.

"I can't do this. It's too depressing," I said, stopping about two hundred feet outside the Basilica. "You go ahead. I'll meet up with you in half an hour."

"Ok. Where?"

"Back at the Best Western or over there."

Sheila followed my gaze across the square to twin golden arches glinting in the sun.

"Ohmygod! Is that what I *think* it is?" she gasped.

Forgetting about her scholarly interest in the Basilica, Sheila yanked my arm and pulled me toward McDonald's.

"Now this, *this* is a fucking miracle," Sheila said. "I've been dying for a burger."

The line at the Lourdes McDonald's – let me say that again, the *Lourdes McDonald's* - was no less reverent than the line at the Basilica. Supplicants stood patiently, waiting to participate in that global communion that comes with a side of fries. Or, in this case, *frites*. Sheila ordered a Quarter-Pounder with cheese, a large order of fries and a jumbo Diet Coke. I just got tea.

"You know, there've been studies done proving that *they* are happier than we are." Sheila's eyes swept the restaurant.

"Who's happier?" I wasn't sure if she meant people who worshipped regularly at the double arches.

"Believers of any religion, the more fanatic the better. They are happier and healthier than the rest of us," Sheila said, creating a puddle of ketchup on her plate. "They feel less pain. They heal faster. They aren't afraid of death so they don't experience as much anxiety or depression."

I found it difficult to take a conversation about health seriously when the speaker was eating a burger made of mystery meat.

"So what's the advantage of being an atheist?" I asked.

Sheila grabbed a fistful of fries.

"Well, we engage in lively debate, drink and screw around without getting morose because we don't believe in Eternal Damnation, and many of us suspect we are not alone here."

"What do you mean we're not alone?"

"This may be just one of a zillion galaxies," Sheila said, expanding her arms to take in all of McDonald's and the Earth spinning silently underneath us. "A lot of astrophysicists, honchos at MIT and NASA, believe that there are *worlds* out there waiting to be discovered."

Sheila spun out scholarly theories on the existence of an ever-expanding universe. She lost me in a linguistic maze of quantum mechanics, chaotic inflation theory and something called Occam's Razor. For a moment, I didn't know which was nuttier, the religious pilgrims who believed in the ecstasy of a 19th century teenager or the NYU professor sitting across from me waiting for the Starship Enterprise to land.

* * * *

Sheila went to the Basilica while I noodled around the town. Then, we took a chair lift 1,000 feet up to the top of Le Pic du Jer. Did I mention I'm afraid of heights? I'm afraid of heights. But the guidebook promised a "stunning" view overlooking Lourdes, Tarbes and the Pyrenées Mountains.

"If you believed in miracles, what would you ask for?" Sheila said.

"Oh, I don't know," I said, imagining the possibilities. Arthur waiting for me at the airport with a bouquet of long-stemmed roses, begging me to forgive him. Making good on my promise to Jacques and finding Nicole's killer before I left France. At this point, either would be miraculous.

"Wanna know what I asked for?" Sheila said.

I looked at her expectantly and waited. Sheila enjoyed the moment.

"I asked for a love muffin. A strong, healthy, *young* man. Not an intellectual. I've had enough of those. He's doesn't have to have an important job either. I just need someone who's fun."

"You asked Saint Bernadette for a love muffin?"

"I certainly did."

"But what's the point in asking if you don't believe?" I asked.

"When you were a kid, did you sit on Santa's lap?"

"Sure. Every kid does."

"Did you stop sitting on Santa's lap when you stopped believing in him?"

"Well, actually, no."

Truth be told, I never stopped sitting on the laps of department store Santas. I borrowed young nieces and nephews so as not to arouse suspicion.

"Exactly my point.

Sheila laughed raucously, causing the chairlift to wobble precariously over the tree tops. Thankful for prayers answered, my feet touched solid ground at the summit where tourists snapped photos in front of a huge cross. It was a crystal clear autumn day and we could see for miles in every direction. Sheila breathed deep of the pure mountain air and held her arms akimbo.

"How can anyone look at this and *not* believe?" she exclaimed.

"In God?"

"No," she said, "In the existence of parallel universes!"

With that, Sheila flung her arms extravagantly, knocking me into an elderly Chinese couple who, in turn, toppled over a cluster of German nuns. There was shouting in a cacophony of languages. People stopped taking photos and ran to the rescue of the hapless pile-up.

To my relief, the Chinese couple, who looked to be 120, did not shatter into a thousand pieces, but slowly stood up and laughed, covering their mouths with their hands, like members of a comedy club audience, delighted to be part of the act. The nuns were not amused. They shot hostile glances at Sheila and me and said things in German that did not sound like benedictions.

"Are you alright?" Sheila asked.

"I guess."

I had fallen on the concrete on my left arm and peeled off my jacket to inspect the damage.

"That doesn't look good." Sheila said.

My arm was red and throbbing from my elbow to my wrist. By the time we got back to the Best Western, it felt like I had stuck my arm in a meat grinder. The flesh that had been red was now turning blue and swelling up. The hotel concierge kindly opened a first-aid kit and provided aspirin, antiseptic and gauze even though I wasn't staying there.

"Ah, we see this all the time," he said. "People come to Lourdes and they are so excited that they don't look where they're going. We have more accidents here than miracles."

I thought he was kidding but in the car on the way back to our hotel, Sheila quoted from the guidebook. "Listen to this," she said, "Even if all of the 4,000 miracles claimed to have happened in Lourdes are true, statistically speaking, more pilgrims have been *fatally* injured than cured."

Now she tells me.

26

When I got back to the hotel, I fashioned a sling out of my bogus Hermes scarf. I knew from high school Red Cross training that keeping my arm immobile was key. It was sprained, not broken, and was responding well to a combination of Advil and Armagnac.

Copper-colored leaves swirled around me as I walked across the park to the brasserie, my jacket draped over my shoulders. The boy I had seen the day I arrived was again pushing his wooden boat in the dry fountain. An elderly woman, his grandmother perhaps, sat on a bench, her head in a book. She looked up as I passed and smiled.

I entered *Le Chien Blanc* and sat at a table next to the window. It was a store-front bistro with blue and white checked café curtains, a counter with six wooden stools and half a dozen tables. Sepia photos of the village from the 1900s hung next to a clock that advertised Kronenbourg Beer. It was too late for the lunch crowd. There were no other customers except a teenager working out his aggressions on a video pinball machine, shouting obscenities, slapping its sides. He had long blue-black hair falling in his eyes, twigs for legs, and a leather jacket with an airbrushed Death's Head on the back.

The place smelled *good* which, of all the qualities to be taken into account when judging an eatery, is the most important. I ordered a *croque monsieur*, not to be mistaken for the American version, a French-toasted ham and American cheese sandwich topped with – agh! - maple syrup. This was the real deal. A split brioche, filled with succulent slices of *jambon de Parme,* in a savory thick cheese sauce with a green salad and glass of red wine. It didn't take more than a few days in France to make me wonder how I ever managed on a slice and a Diet Coke.

While waiting for my platter, I turned the paper placemat into a crime analysis. On one side, I listed *Things I Know* and on the other side *Things I Don't Know*. The *Don't Know* side was much longer. Jacques had provided a motive for Nicole's death, an inconvenient pregnancy and a jealous wife. But Guy de Fondeville, for all his eccentricities, didn't fit the profile of a killer. He discussed Nicole as if she were just one of many tempting chocolates.

And was her pregnancy real or faked? Nicole certainly wasn't "showing" in her short tight skirt. The information would be in the coroner's report which, in Philly, I would've been able to access through my contacts. Here in France, I had no contacts and, from Inspector Beaumonde's point of view, no business poking around. While that might've stopped just about any sane journalist, I welcomed the challenge of flying below the radar.

When my *croquet monsieur* arrived, something rubbed against my leg. I looked under the table. It was the scruffy dog I had previously seen sleeping in the window. It placed its paws on my knees and thumped its tail. I was beginning to realize that the French attitude toward dogs was as passionate as their attitude toward food. Dogs were not only allowed in restaurants, they were welcomed and offered a bowl of water before their owners were served. It seemed that just about every brasserie and bistro had a resident pooch wandering about like a four-legged maitre d'. I dipped a hunk of baguette in cheese sauce, slipped it under the table and gained a dining partner.

Outside, the wind was choreographing autumn's last dance, a mad swirl of color before the landscape puts on its heavy gray winter coat. When I finished eating, I asked the waitress if she sold Gauloise. She didn't. Just as well, I thought. I didn't really want a cigarette I wanted Paul. The taste of his mouth.

Before coming to France, I had read a book of French proverbs. My favorite was, "To reason about love is to lose all reason." At the time, it made me think of Arthur. Now, sitting in a brasserie in Gascony, the proverb applied to my attraction to Paul. To desire him was foolish, inappropriate, unprofessional. Intellectually, I understood. But emotionally, physically, I wanted to rewind the tape to our night of True Lust.

Wordlessly, the pinball aficionado sauntered over to my table, tapped an unfiltered cigarette out of a blue pack, then leaned over and lit my cigarette with his own. Not a day over twenty and enough bravado to start his own revolution. Up close, he was attractive in a Johnny Depp sort of way. Puppy dog eyes, angular jaw, pretty, almost feminine features. Without a word, he went back to the beeps and bells of his demanding mechanical mistress. A few minutes later, he got into a heated conversation with the waitress. He wanted change for the video game and she was reluctant to give it to him. Finally, she slapped a handful of coins on the table.

"*C'est tout, Didi,*" she said, waving her hands in the air.

Didi? There he was, ten feet from me, exactly as Josie had described, right down to the zippers. The motorcycle parked outside was his. If the waitress hadn't called out his name, I might not have put it together, lost as I was in my own murky thoughts. Taking my wine glass and cigarette with me, I walked over where he stood, massaging the pinball machine with his groin.

"Is that your Peugeot?" I asked.

Didi made an affirmative grunt.

"I had a Harley when I was in college. Twelve hundred cc's."

Didi gave me an appraising glance. Actually, I rode on the back of my boyfriend's motorcycle; I couldn't shift gears on a Schwinn.

"Can you show me how to play this thing?" I said, opening my wallet and fishing out a couple of Euros.

"*Oui*" he said, eyeing the Euros, but it came out sounding "way," not "wee," the French version of yeh. Didi stepped aside, showing me where to put the money and how to start the game. I grew up spending summers in the arcades at the Jersey shore and was no stranger to pinball or video games. When it comes to Skee Ball, I am a contender and have a collection of plastic spider rings to prove it.

"How did you hurt your arm?" he asked.

"Mountain climbing," I said, aware that the actual events were irrelevant.

I pretended to be awkward enough to elicit his diligent instruction. Then, I let him beat me to a noisy, flashing crescendo.

"Wow. You're *really* good," I said, "What else do you do for fun around here?"

He gave me a sly smile.

"*Fumez?*" he asked, making a sucking noise with his lips.

He wasn't talking about Gauloise. I hadn't smoked pot since college and often wondered if my generation's passionate embrace of antidepressants and super-caffeinated beverages was a sign of maturity or merely trading up. I followed Didi to a half-timbered house, a short walk from the brasserie. The décor was understated but expensive. *Roset Ligne* sofa, contemporary area rugs, floor to ceiling books, African art.

"Whose house is this?" I asked.

"My parents but they are never home."

"Never?"

"Only on weekends. They keep an apartment in Toulouse."

Didi's father worked in the aerospace industry, his mother was a psychologist. He led me to his room, black walls covered with punk rock posters. The only furniture was a mattress on the floor, covered in purple sheets that could use a wash. I stood in the doorway while he expertly rolled a fat joint. Didi lit up, inhaled and extended the it in my direction. He then put on French rap which sounded better than American rap, if only because I couldn't understand the words. When he leaned over and offered me a "shot gun," I declined. If you've never done it, think of mouth-to-mouth resuscitation but shooting smoke, rather than oxygen, into the recipient's lungs.

"I thought you wanted to have *fun*," he said, "Take off your jacket. Relax."

"Didi, I am old enough to be…."

"You think I haven't been with a woman your age? I prefer older women. At least they know what they want. Young girls, they are so stupid. So ignorant. They disgust me."

He took a drag and held it out in my direction. I took a hit – for purely medicinal reasons.

"But there must be many girls your age around here who are charming, intelligent… and *fun*," I said.

"They are all stupid cows," he said, resting his head in my lap, as if it were the most natural thing in the world. Didi, short for Didier, was handsome and as self-assured as a blackjack dealer. If I were twenty years younger, my legs would've been in the air by now.

"What about that pretty blond who worked in the hotel?"

"Nicole? What about her?"

"Well, she seemed to have a certain….sense of style."

Didi's faced scrunched up as if he had tasted something bitter.

"She was a dumb cunt."

"So you knew her?"

"I fucked her. We got high a couple of times. What difference does it make?" His upper lip started to twitch.

"It's so sad. She was only twenty-one." I said.

"She was nineteen."

The details came out. Nicole had been the first girl to introduce him to the addiction of unrequited love and other substances. She had a supply of heroin from Marseilles and recruited Didi as her sales rep. The throbbing in my arm went away. There really is something to be said for the pain management attributes of good pot. Or even mediocre pot.

"Nicole didn't use drugs. Not even pot. It was all about the money," Didi said. "We were supposed to go to Paris. That was the plan."

Didi spoke so softly I almost couldn't hear him. "I couldn't leave without telling my mother. She said Nicole had mental problems. She called her a sociopath. My mother has a name for everyone who does not conform to her *milieu*."

"What did you do?"

"I broke up with Nicole. I didn't answer her calls. A few days later, she was dead."

"It wasn't your fault, Didi."

"How do you know?"

He looked at me with huge, dilated pupils through a cloud of smoke. Didi turned up the volume of the music, nodding his head in time to the beat. *THUMP! THUMP! THUMP! THUMP!* In every exchange of information, there is a moment when you need to decide how many cards to put on the table, in hopes of picking up one of greater value. I decided to throw my Ace.

"Did you know Nicole was pregnant?"

"It wasn't mine," he said a bit too quickly. "We used condoms almost every time."

This wasn't the moment to inform Didi that there is no such thing as "almost" pregnant.

"Do you know whose baby it was?" I asked.

His lip started to twitch again. "Why are you asking me?"

"I am trying to help a friend of Nicole, someone who may be falsely accused of her murder."

Didi jumped up off the bed.

"Not me! I wasn't here. I was in Toulouse that night."

"No, Didi. Not you. There is someone else who cared very much about Nicole and who wants to make sure the murderer is caught. You understand?"

"Not really. I didn't think anyone cared about Nicole...," his voiced dropped to a whisper, "....except me."

I put my arm around his shoulder. His hair smelled sweetly of marijuana.

"Think hard, Didi. Even if it doesn't seem that important, anything you remember could help."

"Nicole liked to go to Biarritz to play with rich, old men like a cat plays with a mouse. She prowled the casinos. When she brought men luck, they bought her things, designer clothes, jewelry. "

Didi stretched languidly, closed his eyes and seemed to doze off.

How many times had I fallen for that when I was in my twenties? The exaggerated yawn, the sleepy eyes, the rumpled sheets.

"I better be going." I jumped up and was half way out the door.

"If you need anything...I can get it for you," he called after me.

"Like what?" I stuck my head back in the room.
"Weed, pharmaceuticals, whatever you want."
"Good to know."

27

"How's your arm?" Sheila asked.

"Better."

I had recruited Sheila to help me review Château Mignon's cuisine for my article. Having my arm in a sling and wondering when Paul would reappear had lowered my appetite and Sheila was well-suited to the task. She plowed through a large crock of onion soup, artichokes vinaigrette and emitted satisfied grunts, smacking her lips. I wanted to keep the conversation focused on the food, but Sheila kept circling back to my career change.

"I'm no Freudian, far from it," she said, looking up from her platter of *canard a l'orange* with *purée de pommes de terre* and *petit pois.* "But I believe that ninety percent of the choices we make are rooted deep in our subconscious. All those years you spent reporting on domestic violence and the victimization of women, there must've been some pivotal event that drew you to the subject."

If Sheila was thinking I witnessed violence as a child or in my marriage, she had been in academia too long. Even her small talk sounded like a midterm.

"I mean, you could've reported on politics, economics or health. Why domestic violence?" Sheila asked.

"When I was in college, my roommate was fished out of the Schuylkill River. Her death was initially ruled a suicide even though there was evidence of blunt force trauma. We all knew her boyfriend did it but his family had connections, enough to help him flee the country before the D.A. could convene a grand jury. Before her murder, I had wanted to be an entertainment reporter. Afterward, it seemed so trivial. I did an internship in investigative reporting and got my masters at Columbia before starting at the *Daily Star*."

"Did they ever catch the bastard?"

"No. He's been spotted in Uruguay, Stockholm, East Berlin. But he always evades capture. For all I know, he's right here in the Midi Pyrenees and Nicole is his latest victim."

* * * *

Now it was my turn. I asked Sheila what attracted her to gender studies.

"Adam Krupnick. I was an undergrad at Columbia. Adam was chair of the gender studies department. The first time our eyes met it was True Fuck. We did it in the stacks, the faculty lounge. One time, in a stairwell. Of course, that was back when I had a figure you would not believe. Oh, don't look so shocked. Your generation didn't invent sex."

"He was your professor. He took advantage of you."

"Good god, no. We were two consenting adults. This was before all the PC crapola. Students got high with professors, had sex with them. It was the norm. Now if I invite a student for coffee, I have to worry."

"I thought you were a feminist."

"I am but I don't want to take liberties away from either sex. Men and women should be equally empowered and *paid* without the feds telling us what we can and can't do with our bodies."

My original impression of Sheila took a one-eighty. Behind her frumpy appearance and Bronx bark was a facile mind. I was fascinated by her ability to leapfrog all over a conversation, jumping from topic to topic, from the philosophic to the banal.

"Sexuality is something that can't be legislated," she continued, "But, from the beginning of time, governments and religions have been trying to control it. *Thou shall. Thou shalt not.* When women are murdered, in most cases, it's by someone they know intimately. From what I hear, this Nicole babe was hot to trot," said Sheila. "Add an unwanted pregnancy and drugs and I'd say her murder was inevitable. What I don't get is her relationship with the hunchback."

"Jacques is not a hunchback. He just has some kind of facial paralysis. Once you get to know him, he has a certain rough charm."

"Charm? Let me get this. Some thug grabs you out of your hotel room, holds you hostage, demands ransom and you're *charmed?* Sounds like Stockholm Syndrome to me."

"I'm just trying to be objective. Jacques acted out of fear, desperation. The police always suspect the fiancé."

"For good reason," Sheila countered, "One, you say this Jacques character crashed Fondeville's party looking for a fight. Two, you found him dead drunk outside. Three, the guy's got motivation, access and intent."

"You sound like *Law and Order*."

"My brother-in-law works for the NYPD. He says the only difference between what happens on the street and on TV is the pay scale. Listen, if Jacques didn't start the fire, accidentally or on purpose, who did?"

"I don't know. There were torches leading from the Château through the woods to the parking area. Maybe the wind knocked one over."

"Or arson."

No way. I could not place the destruction of a magnificent château and vineyard in the same category as a torched warehouse in Hoboken.

Madame Picard wheeled over the dessert cart. Sheila had chocolate mousse garnished with candied violets and I had a pear tart with whipped cream. I had lost my appetite, not my sanity.

"This little violet once had political clout." Sheila said, holding a tiny sugared flower between her thumb and forefinger. "The Parma violet was originally brought from Italy to France by Napoleon's troops. When Napoleon and Josephine went into exile in Elba, the violet became the symbol of the Bonapartists. They wore purple clothes to show their support. Having violets in your garden was a political statement."

Oy, another unsolicited lecture.

"What's your overall impression of the food?" I asked, attempting to steer Sheila back to her dining experience.

Sheila shrugged her shoulders and rolled her eyes.

"If you like French, it's okay. Right now, I would kill for some moo shoo pork."

That wasn't the quote I was seeking. I would have to wheedle an interview out of Madame Picard. Considering my previous encounters with her, that would take a bit of ingenuity. So after desert and coffee, when Madame offered us her homemade violet liqueur, I sang its praises as if it were an elixir of the Gods.

"*Merci. Merci beaucoup, mademoiselle,*" Madame trilled. "The secret recipe has been in my family for generations. Many of our guests buy our liqueur as a souvenir."

"What a charming idea," I gushed, "I'd love to buy some. Wouldn't you Sheila?"

I kicked Sheila under the table.

"Ouch. Yeh, sure. Give me a bottle too."

"*Avec plaisir, mademoiselle,*" Madame sang happily and toddled away.

"Why the hell did you do that? This stuff tastes like poison," Sheila protested.

"I want to get on her good side."

"That old bitch? She doesn't have one," Sheila said, pushing her liqueur aside.

I debated about telling Sheila what I was doing after dinner. But the investigative reporter in me needed to let someone know my whereabouts, in case something went wrong. I couldn't tell Paul and Inspector Beaumonde was out of the question.

"I'm going to Château des Rêves tonight," I admitted. "I want to have a look around and figure out the connection between the fire and Nicole's murder."

"Suppose his wife is there?"

"She's out of town."

"How do you know?"

"I've got sources."

Actually, all I had was Didi, who passed along what he heard and provided transportation on the back of his motorcycle when needed in exchange for beer and pinball money.

"No fuckin' way," Sheila said, causing the couple at the adjacent table to shoot her a withering glance. "You are not going there…"

"Sheila, I appreciate your concern but…"

"You're interrupting. Let me finish."

I gritted my teeth. Sheila continued.

"As I was saying, you are not going there by *yourself*. I am going with you."

Her suggestion was absurd. I patiently ticked off all the reasons this was not going to happen.

"What I am going to do is illegal and, if I'm caught, I could end up as a permanent guest of the French prison system. I'll take responsibility for myself, but not for you."

"So I should sit on my *tuchis* and die of fucking boredom?" she said in a voice that filled the entire dining room. "I'll take what's behind door number two, thank you."

28

Our taxi driver was a woman with hair the color of eggplant. She kept the radio on a station that played country western music, Gascon style. She spoke the local patois and seemed to think that if she spoke louder we would understand. Between the music and her shouting, I was thankful to get out of the car at Château des Rêves. The driver poked her head out the window, "*Oooh la la.* This is the château that burned."

"*Oui, oui,*" I said, following her eyes. The fire had scorched half the château, draping a black shroud over its pink walls. The courtyard was littered with amputated tree limbs.

"We won't be long. Wait for us here," I instructed the driver.

"You think she's going to wonder why we are visiting when no one's home?" Sheila asked.

"Nah. As long as the meter's running, she'll have no complaints."

Sheila stood by the front door as primly as a Seventh Day Adventist while I entered through a side window that had been blown open during the fire. I used a mini halogen flashlight to find the light switch. My boots squished down on the water-logged carpet, my nostrils flinched at the acrid stench. Carcasses of 18th century settees and Louis XIV chairs were belly up, showing their moldy innards. I opened the front door for Sheila.

"*Oy, oy, oy,*" she muttered, looking around, "What a waste!"

Sheila confined herself to the first floor while I went upstairs. In the master bedroom, drawers and closets were flung open like a robbery in progress. A large grey rectangle on the wall indicated where the nude painting had hung. Sent out for restoration? I looked under the bed, inside shoe boxes, all the places where husbands and wives hide secrets from one another. I found nothing more incriminating than a cache of department store receipts stuffed inside an evening purse.

The adjoining sitting room contained an art nouveau walnut writing desk; it was either an authentic Gallé or a damn good reproduction. The desk contained the usual assortment of stationery, writing implements, stamps and notepads. Nothing out of the ordinary. One drawer didn't open. It required a key. I didn't have a key and I didn't have time. God and *Architectural Digest* forgive me, but I heaved the desk over.

The drawer flew open. Packets of correspondence tumbled out. Postcards and blue airmail letters with feathery handwriting, Christmas cards, all neatly bundled. The oldest correspondence, postmarked Marseille, was tied with a pink ribbon. I couldn't decipher the handwriting. European script looks like lace to me. What caught my attention were Christmas cards signed "Nikki" in a childish scrawl. A photo of a little girl fell out of a card. She had blond hair and a wistful smile. My brain did jumping jacks. Could little Nikki be Nicole?

Reading Sandrine's mail and checking the dates on the postmarks, it seemed that Nikki was born when Sandrine was sixteen. The letters were not addressed to "mama" but still. This threw a wrench into my theory that Nicole was the victim of a love triangle gone wrong. I could imagine Sandrine killing her husband's lover out of jealousy. But if Nicole was her daughter, it didn't make sense. I stuffed the packet of letters into my jeans.

In Sandrine's bathroom, the syringes were gone. The box they came in was in the wastebasket along with three empty vials. Each vial had the same label, Didrex, and a different prescribing doctor. I didn't know what Didrex was, but if Sandrine was getting it from three different doctors, it had to be a controlled substance.

I ran downstairs to find Sheila sitting at the kitchen table, spreading *foie gras* on a cracker, her prodigious chest flecked with crumbs, a glass of white wine at hand. I set the vials on the table.

"What's that?" she asked.

"I don't know," I said, reading the fine print on a vial. "Some kind of injectable drug."

Sheila dipped a knife into the foie gras.

"Have a nosh," she said, "It's delish."

"Sheila, put that away."

"If I were home, I'd be having my late snack now," she whined.

"Well, you're *not* home."

There was a loud hammering on the front door. *BANG! BANG! BANG!*

"Shit. Our driver is getting antsy, c'mon," I said, then shouted toward the door, "We're coming. We're coming."

When I opened the door, I was blinded by the high beams of a car. It wasn't our taxi. It was the police.

29

"Why are they making such a *tsimmis*? It's not like we were stealing."
Sheila said.

"We were trespassing."

"I'll replace the godamn *foie gras*," she grumbled, "Where the hell
are they taking us?"

Calming Sheila was futile. She fed on adversity, a true adrenaline
junkie. Her cheeks flushed. Her eyes glistened.

"The guy in the passenger seat is adorable," she purred.

The police officers had asked to see our identification but had not
bothered to inspect our handbags. The paté in Sheila's purse would
evoke no more than a raised brow. It was the empty vials in my
pocket that worried me. I was tempted to toss them out the window.
But they may have been all that stood between Jacques and a jail cell.

"Where are we going?" Sheila asked in heavily Bronx-accented
French.

"To the *Commissariat de Police*," said the baby-faced cop in the
passenger seat.

Sheila turned to me. "I don't like this. It's almost midnight. They
could throw us in jail till the day shift starts."

Tempting as it was, I did not remind Sheila that accompanying me
to the Fondeville's Château was her idea. I pretended to be fascinated
by what I could see out the window. Absolutely nothing. The
commissariat was located in a former Renaissance mansion in Auch.
Its expansive rooms had been sliced and diced to accommodate the
needs of the regional police headquarters, filled with metal file
cabinets and the drone of fax machines, printers and office chatter.

We were directed to a row of chairs in a hallway next to a water cooler. It smelled like a police station, a disheartening mix of stale coffee, tobacco and despair. All that remained of the mansion's original glory were the cracked marble floors, gilded ceiling and a faded fresco depicting *The Rape of Europa.*

"I was born in the wrong century," sighed Sheila, gazing at the abundantly fleshed female nudes in the fresco. "The concept of the ideal female has transmuted from a strong, full-figured woman who could plow the fields and march into battle into an androgynous weakling. Can you imagine Kate Moss firing an AK-47? She probably requires assistance to pick up a fork."

Sheila was just warming to her topic when the younger of the two police officers reappeared.

"Inspector Beaumonde will speak with you now," he said.

The Inspector's office was a high-ceilinged, windowless box devoid of décor, save for a soccer calendar. Sheila and I sat in hard wooden chairs while Beaumonde shuffled papers as if we were invisible. He finally looked up at us in bewilderment.

"Mademoiselle Woof? Madame Schlossberg?"

"Schlossberg-*Koon*," Sheila corrected him.

"How did you injure your arm?" he asked me.

"It happened at Lourdes…"

Beaumonde cut me off , "The taxi driver stated that you went to Château des Rêves for the purpose of retrieving a lost necklace?"

That was my story and I was sticking to it.

"Yes, I lost it Saturday night at the dinner party."

Beaumonde made a notation. "And you entered the Château through a window?"

"Well, yes, but…"

"I entered through the front door," Sheila added, unhelpfully.

"You are aware that your presence inside the Fondeville's château constitutes a violation of the law?"

"Inspector, may I speak to you alone?" I asked.

Sheila threw me a sulky look, then hoisted herself out of her chair with a grunt. When she noisily closed the door behind her, I continued.

"When I attended the Armagnac Producers' gala at Château des Rêves. Baron de Fondeville gave me a personal tour of his château. He wanted to show me his art collection. The other guests were outside. The tour included rooms on the second floor. Bedrooms...."

Beaumonde shifted in his chair impatiently. "*S'il vous plait, Madame*. Make your point."

"Monsieur Fondeville attacked me in his bedroom. That's where I lost my necklace. So, you see, I couldn't really ask Madame Fondeville if she found it. It would be insensitive, given the Baron's recent death."

Beaumonde rubbed his temples and squeezed his eyes shut. When he opened them, he seemed disappointed to find I was still there.

"Did you find your necklace?" he asked.

"No. I did not."

"I see. Please put your purse on my desk and remove all of its contents."

My purse was a magenta tote bag imprinted with *The Daily Star* logo, a five-pointed star over the Philly skyline. It was big enough to hold a change of clothing, six large hoagies (with everything) and Mongo. Which explained its persistent odor of onions, mayo and meow. I dumped the contents on the Inspector's desk. Notepad, roller ball pens, Tic Tacs, Kleenex, Super Tampax, Advil, cell phone, wallet, Double Chocolate Milanos, a clotted hairbrush. Two lipsticks rolled out. Mine and the one that had been worn by the Baron. I had no intention of using it, purples made me look like a zombie, but I hadn't thrown it away yet.

"*C'est tout?*" he asked, as if expecting me to pull out an Uzi.

I pulled the vials out of my jacket pocket, along with the photo of the little blond girl.

The Inspectors eyebrows arched in disapproval.

"Inspector, I am not a thief. I am a journalist."

"*Oui. Oui.* A journalist," he said icily, "A journalist who trespasses on private property. You have no right to this photo or to anything inside Château des Rêves."

"I was only trying to help your investigation of the death of Nicole and Baron Fondeville. I found these drugs bathroom in Madame de Fondeville's bathroom, I believe this is a controlled substance and..."

"Enough! " he yelled, slapping his hand hard on the desk. "I do not need your *help*. Whatever information you have was gathered without authority."

From his tone, I figured I would soon find out if "bread and water" in France meant baguettes and Perrier.

"Am I under arrest?" I asked.

Beaumonde cracked his fingers, enjoying his moment.

"I spoke with Madame de Fondeville. She does not wish to charge you with trespassing..." Beaumonde said with a trace of regret. "However, you are to have no further contact with her. You are not permitted to go to her château or to contact her ever again."

I wagged my head like a kid in the principal's office and shoved my belongings back into my carryall. When I got to the Baron's lipstick, my thoughts raced out of my mouth before I could shove them back inside.

"This lipstick belonged to Baron de Fondeville. Nicole worn the same shade." I said. "You need to have it tested."

The Inspector looked at me as if maggots were crawling out of my mouth.

"*Quel absurdité?*"

I rattled on. It was past midnight and I was past I loopy.

"It was manufactured at Chateau des Reves. See, this is their coat of arms, the heart with two swords. It contains Armagnac, but it could also contain some kind of lethal poison."

"Slow down, *Mademoiselle.*" Beaumonde raised his palms at me. "How did this *rouge à lèvres* come into your possession?"

"When I went to the hotel in Vic-Fezensac with the Baron, he had the lipstick with him."

"With him? How do you mean? "

I had a choice. Preserve the Baron's dignity or catch his killer and remove suspicion from myself. I went for the twofer.

"The Baron put this lipstick on in the hotel room. It belonged to him."

The Inspector did not flinch. I wasn't sure if he was even breathing.

"Then how come my men did not find any traces of *leepsteek* on the Baron? How come it is *your* possession, *Mademoiselle*?

Oh, this wasn't going well at all.

"I know how this sounds but I washed the Baron's face and removed the lipstick before the police arrived. When you found his cosmetics in the bathroom, I told you they were mine to protect his reputation."

The Inspector folded his arms and gave me the dead mackerel look again.

"Why should I believe that this *leepsteek* belonged to the Baron and not to you? It's preposterous! Unless he gave it to you as a gift? That is the only logical explanation."

"Since when do sexual appetites conform to logic, Inspector? If I hadn't washed the Baron's face before you arrived, you would've found this lipstick on his mouth."

"Which could've happened from kissing you."

"And the mascara, eye shadow and rouge? Look, I know it's wrong to tamper with a death scene. I'm sorry I did it, I panicked. But my gut tells me that this lipstick might hold the key to the death of the Baron and Nicole."

He pushed his chair back and let out a long puff of air.

"Poison lipstick? That is quite an imaginative story. The only part of which I am certain is that you were the first person to discover the body of Nicole Tomas and you were with Guy de Fondeville when he died. Now you admit to not only trespassing on private property but to withholding evidence." He picked up the lipstick, removed the cap and sniffed. "*Pas mal.* I will indulge your fantasy and send this to the lab."

He gathered up the vials and the photo of the little girl. "These items will be returned to Madame Fondeville." He cleared his throat. "I hope you understand the gravity of the situation. You have made yourself an annoyingly consistent factor in the investigation of two suspicious deaths and one of the most destructive fires we have had here in years. If we meet again, *mademoiselle,* it will not be pleasant."

Beaumonde didn't say *au revoir* for the obvious reasons. I stood up, I felt the crunch of the letters that I had stuffed into my jeans, and willed them to stay put as I left his office.

30

While I was being interrogated, Sheila had made a date with the baby-faced policeman.

"Research for my next book, "*Sex, Lies & Aging,*" she said.

Sheila clearly enjoyed our police escort back to the hotel.

"Hey, wasn't there something missing from your hotel room?" I asked as we tooled through the empty streets of Auch.

"Oh, yeh, my watch. I'll file an insurance claim."

She didn't sound terrible concerned. She was too busy flirting with Baby Cop. I, on the other hand, had no intention of going home without my wedding ring. When we arrived back at the hotel, the door was locked. We stood, huddled in the darkened entryway like delinquent teenagers, waiting for Picard. He finally let us in, but not before throwing a deeply aggrieved glance at the idling police van.

It was late, I was exhausted, but did not go to sleep. I booted up my laptop and emailed Gabriella. I told her about my missing ring and asked her to consult with her *orishas* to get it back. It was 2 a.m. in France, 7 p.m. yesterday in Philly. My grandmother would be reigning over the dinner table, forcing second and third helpings on adult children whom, if they ate another serving of her pulled pork, would go into cardiac arrest. Did I believe her Santeria spells would find my wedding ring? Not really. It was my way of sending my grandmother a long-distance hug and letting her know she was important to me.

I did a Google search for Didrex. It was an amphetamine. Speed, "used for diet control in obese individuals." So that's why Sandrine was as thin and as high strung as an Afghan hound. Probably started using it as a young model and never kicked the habit. Interestingly, Didrex was taken off the market in France several years ago because of accidental deaths. That raised the question. How did she get the drug? Perhaps that is what fueled Sandrine's frequent trips to Paris. Not designer shoes, but designer drugs.

*   *   *   *

BRRRRRRRING……BRRRRING…..BRRRING.   I stretched my good arm out from under the covers, grabbed the receiver and slammed it back down, thinking it was my wakeup call.   I slipped back into dreamland.   A minute later, it rang again. What the *hell*?   I put the receiver to my ear and barked, "YES?"

"I am in the lobby."

It was Paul. I sprang up in bed. AGGGH! My back felt like it had been worked over with a jack hammer. I must've twisted it the wrong way when I climbed through the window.

"Did I wake you? It's almost noon." Paul asked.

I searched for my fully awake, professional voice. What came out was a squeaky toad.

"No, no. I'm just getting a cold. I'll be right down. "

No time for a shower.   I blended moisturizer and cream blush between my palms, then slapped it all over my face. An old mortician's trick that puts a healthy glow on the dead. I pulled on jeans and a turtleneck. I threw a parting glance at the mirror. French women never wear under-eye concealer. They prefer to look *très fatiguée,* as if they stayed up all night having sex. I didn't look like I had had sex. I looked like I had gone two rounds with Mike Tyson.

Paul was in the lobby, his laptop open on his knees, a cell phone pressed to his ear. He held up a finger, ended his conversation, stood and brushed his cheeks against mine. An empty cup was on the table next to his chair. I gazed at it enviously. I needed a pot of coffee. Intravenously.

"What happened to you?" he asked, staring at my fashionable sling.

"It's a souvenir from my visit to Lourdes."

Paul stifled a smile.

"I've drawn up a schedule," he said, handing me a list of vineyards and attractions within an hour's drive of the hotel. "If there are no, ah, further distractions, we should be done in two days."

He was all business. Paul was there to work, not to get *involved.* Not with me and, most certainly not with the police investigation into the murder of Nicole. If he had known that I had taken an involuntary tour of the *Commissarriat,* Paul would've run the four-minute mile back to Toulouse.

"D'accord? You agree?" he asked.

"Yes, on one condition."

Paul stiffened.

"Can I have some coffee first?"

* * * *

We went to Briat Vineyard. It had a lovely country manor house, a castle really, built in 1540 by Queen Jeanne d'Albert as a hunting lodge in Mauvezin d'Armagnac. I wondered if queens really hunted? Or did they simply lie about their country estates reading the medieval version of *Vogue*, drinking Chardonnay and ordering the kids to "go outside and play" like the rest of us? I was more interested in the interior décor of the château than in its celebrated Armagnac. But like a good soldier, I marched on and sampled my fair share of brandy.

"You're drinking it too fast," Paul said, taking a glass out of my hand. "Warm it first like this."

He swirled the crystal snifter slowly between his hands.

"Then inhale, don't drink," he instructed. "Now taste, but don't swallow. Let it roll around your tongue."

Paul wasn't trying to be seductive, but telling me what to do with my tongue was a bit much.

"You're not wearing your wedding ring," he said.

"I lost it."

"Quel dommage."

"It's warm in here," I said, "I'm gonna get some air."

As I walked outside into fizzy the autumn sunlight, my cell phone played the opening bars of *Some Enchanted Evening.* The tune was ironic and urbane when I was with Arthur. Without him, it was accusatory. I didn't recognize the caller ID. It was Jacques.

"You must go back to Château des Rêves," he said.

"That is not possible. Inspector Beaumonde said..."

"Listen to me. Go back to the château. Go to the cellar. There is a storage room in the back, next to my office. The key is under my desk. Inside the storage room you will find proof of who set the fire."

Why the hell didn't he tell me this before? His voice was clear, as if he were nearby.

"Where are you?"

Jacques hung up. If told Beaumonde what Jacques said, the Inspector would not take me seriously. If anything, he'd lock me up.

"*Ça va?*"

I spun around. Paul was next to me. How long had he been there? I slipped my phone back into my bag.

"We should leave now if we want to get to Auch for lunch," Paul announced.

Auch? I grimaced, thinking of my recent visit to the Commissariat, but my fears were misplaced. The restaurant, *Le Jardin des Saveurs,* was located in a frothy, whipped cream cake of a building across from the statue of D'Artagnan.

"The chef, Roland Garreau, is the best in the Midi," Paul said, kissing his fingertips.

Crystal chandeliers glittered above. Starched waiters glided by silently, as if on roller skates. The maitre d' greeted Paul warmly and showed us to a table. The chairs were upholstered in sunflower yellow leather, crisply starched white table linens were double-draped down to the floor. This was, by far, the most formal restaurant we had visited. I wished Paul had warned me. Female patrons were swathed in silk and cashmere on a weekday afternoon. I was in jeans and a leather jacket.

"They know me here," Paul whispered.

Gazing at the prices on the menu, I wondered how Paul managed to be a regular.

"You come here often?" I asked.

"When someone else is picking up the tab."

Paul ordered as if it was his last meal: foie gras, roasted duck Maigret, steamed vegetables, salad, cheeses. I ordered food I could eat with a fork, without the aid of my left hand. Cocktails appeared, *kir royale*, followed by regional wines. When our entrées arrived, Paul handled his knife and fork deftly, like surgical instruments, maintaining perfect posture and a slow, methodical pace.

French dining etiquette bares no resemblance to the free-for-all meals of my childhood where food flew through the air as readily as conversation. In my family, talking with a full mouth was a necessity, if you wanted to get in a word. Europeans don't juggle utensils from hand to hand as we do. The fork never leaves the left hand. The knife stays firmly in the right. And when they take a bite, a small bite mind you, the head turns just so. I smiled to myself imagining Paul at Gabriella's table, delicately pecking his way through her *pollo con arroz*.

Paul chatted more with the sommelier than with me. There was no flirtation, no exchange of personal confidences, just the necessary acknowledgements. More wine? How's the veal? *Ça va?* Only a few days ago, we had Historic Sex, now this. I was a little drunk, a little sleepy and very horny. I reached for Paul's hand.

"Paul, I'm really sorry about…."

He pulled his hand away.

"*De rien…* We have work to do."

A waiter swept crumbs off the table using a silver-handled brush, his eyes alert as if dusting for fingerprints. On my side of the table, the linen was littered with crumbs and stained with wine spots and salad dressing. Paul's side was immaculate.

* * * *

Our next stop was Condom. No, really. Long before the word became synonymous with awkward teenage sex, the town of Condom was a stop along the pilgrimage route to Santiago de Compostela. No one snickered then and Paul didn't crack a smile now as we passed a road sign.. Maybe that's because the word for penis raincoats in French isn't condom, it's *préservatif.*

According to my guidebook, bawdy associations with the town's name caused tourists to steal street signs, so the town fathers decided to cash in and opened a birth control museum. We didn't go there, thank God. We went to Chateau Cassaigne, an armagnac vineyard built by the Abbot of Condom in the 13th century.

No wonder the Cathars questioned the excesses of the Church. This was no humble abode. The chateau was a veritable palace containing a vast armagnac cellar, the original medieval kitchen (I suspect there was a spiffy modern kitchen with a complete set of Le Creuset Cookware that was off-limits to tourists) and an impressive botanical garden. Except for a brief stab at sharing the wealth during the Revolution, the sumptuous chateau and sprawling vineyard were still owned by descendants of the Abbot of Condom. *Le plus ca change…*

Paul handed me off to a guide, a perky young blond, and vanished. The guide deposited me in a dark room, in front of a video screen that told the story of Chateau Cassaigne on a repeating seven-minute loop. It was in black and white, narrated by an Englishman, which gave it the feel of a PBS documentary. No one was viewing the film but me, alone on a wooden bench. My mind wandered as images of happy peasants harvesting grapes in the 1920s flickered like a silent film. Was Paul distant because I jumped to the wrong conclusion when I saw his photos of Nicole? Or was he playing it cool, make that cold, because I was right?

When I arrived at the Tasting Room, another perky blond was waiting with a tray of empty brandy snifters and a selection of armagnacs. Paul was already there, chatting her up and sampling her wares. I wasn't imaging it. Paul was purposefully ignoring me. I sipped and spit, not concentrating on the brandy's "nose" or it's "bloom" but on the gentle cascade of Paul's conversation with the sommelier in medieval wench garb: white peasant blouse, laced black bustier, full green skirt.

"Why don't you come outside with me? There's a herd of deer on the grounds that would make a great photo for the article," I said.

"I got it. You go ahead," he said.

31

The male ego. Never sell it short. In spite of Paul keeping me at arm's length the entire day, he behaved like a jealous lover that evening when Didi showed up at the hotel, kissed me on both cheeks and handed me a helmet.

"*Au revoir*," I said to Paul and, without further explanation, followed Didi out to his motorcycle. He climbed onto his Peugeot. I swung my leg over the seat and wrapped my one good arm lightly around Didi's slender waist.

"Who was that?" Didi asked, turning on the engine.

"A photographer I'm working with."

"*C'est tout*? That's all?"

"Why?"

Didi turned towards me.

"He looked at me like I was taking something that belongs to him. Am I?"

I shook my head and smiled, noticing a cigarette glowing in the dark by the hotel entrance. The thought that Paul could be standing there watching us made me feel like a teenager sneaking out of the house for a date with a bad influence. Didi lit up a joint and passed it to me. I declined. One of us had to remain sober. I had told Did I was bored, true enough, and wanted to experience whatever passed for nightlife in Gascony. I also made it clear I would pick up the tab.

"You like jazz?" he asked.

"*Oui, oui*," I said, expecting not much more than a village bar with a trio of trained chimps banging out standards.

Didi took a zigzag route along narrow country roads, avoiding the main thoroughfare. I hadn't been on a bike in almost fifteen years but it all came back to me, leaning into the curves, keeping my weight centered, making love to the wind. I had a huge smile plastered on my face. I was happy in that idiotic way people are when they get off a roller coaster or the New Jersey Turnpike.

A half hour later, we arrived at L'Atelier, a jazz club in Marciac. I readjusted my estimation of the club and Didi. L'Atelier was a contemporary nightclub restaurant with a young, hip crowd, a first rate jazz band and, from the aroma hanging in the air, good things happening in the kitchen. The host greeted Didi warmly and guided us to a table. Didi introduced me as *"mon ami,"* draped a territorial arm around my shoulder and held my chair when we got to our table. Josie was right. Didi was a good guy.

"Do you come here often?" I asked.

"Since I was a child. My father is a jazz guitarist. Being an engineer is just his day job. Sometimes he sits in with the band. I grew up listening to Django Rheinhardt, Stephan Grappelli, Jean Lu Ponty, Astrid Gilberto."

"Gilberto, really? Do you like her daughter Bebel?"

"She's cool. But I prefer the music from Bahia, the *tropicalismo* of Caetano Veloso and the baticada of Olodum."

I was stunned. Brazilian jazz is one of my passions. Arthur dubbed me a Brazil Nut and did his Carmen Miranda imitation whenever I got excited about a new Veloso CD or daydreamed about going to Rio. And here was this kid, young enough to be my son, discussing the fine points of Brazilian jazz. He not only knew the music, but had seen an incredible number of jazz artists perform live.

"They're here every summer at the Marciac Jazz Festival. Last year, I saw Diana Krall, Wynton Marsalis, Chick Corea and Gilbetto Gil."

Didi bopped his head appreciatively to the Coltrane sax solo. I had thought I was in Sleepy Hollow. Turns out that the Midi Pyrenees was awash in music and art festivals from May through September, the French version of the Newport Jazz Festival.

Didi ordered for us both. *Floc de Gascogne* aperitifs, the Gascon version of a wine cooler consisting of grape juice and brandy, then a zippy gazpacho followed by *tajine*, a North African stew of goose, apricots and almonds, served in a decorative conical clay dish.

"*Ça va?*" Didi asked as I sopped up the *tajine* sauce with a hunk of bread.

"*Superbe.*"

Didi explained that the exotic dish was almost as common in the Midi as cassoulet, due to the proximity to North Africa and the large number of Algerian immigrants. Looking around, I noticed a fair number of patrons and staff had the darker complexion and gazelle eyes of North Africa and Spain. Coming from Philly, I'm at home in an ethnically diverse ambience, and don't know quite what to make of places where everyone looks like they were cloned from the same zygote.

"Is the band local?" I asked.

"*Oui.* They are from Toulouse. Terrific, no?"

They were terrific, yes. For the past week, I had been seduced by the cuisine and brandy of Gascony. Now I was adding a third element. Live music. I felt as if I had broken through the tourist barrier and was finally experiencing southwest France like a native. Not that the vineyards, museums and restaurants I had visited with Paul were tourists traps, far from it. But L'Atlerier was exactly the kind of place where I'd be on Saturday night if I lived in the Midi. Not with a twenty-year-old, of course. Not even a soignée one like Didi. I had the distinct impression that he liked being seen with an older woman.

When the band took a break, I steered the conversation toward Didi's pharmaceutical sideline, hoping to find some sort of connection between him and Sandrine de Fondeville.

"You said you could get anything. What do you have that will help me lose weight?"

Didi scowled.

"You don't need to lose weight. You're fine."

Compliments will get you everywhere.

"Not a lot. Just a little." I said.

"You sound like my mother."

Oy. I threw my hair over one shoulder.

"Do you have amphetamines, speed?"

Didi moved his chair closer to mine.

"I'll ask around. Now that Nicole is… I'm not really in that business anymore. Just pot, hash and ecstasy. I'm thinking of going back to school, studying industrial design."

"When you were in… that business…did you sell a drug called Didrex?"

His eyes met mine for an instant, then looked away.

"I've heard of it." He laid one finger on the inside of my elbow. For a moment, I didn't understand then I got it. Injectable.

"Yes," I said.

"Give me a few days. But you know, there is a better way to stay in shape."

I raised my eyebrows.

"Make love," he said, combing my hair with his fingers.

I wanted to laugh but Didi gathered my hair into his hand at the nape of my neck, then gave it a twist, angling my mouth towards his. It happened so fast, I didn't have time to think, much less pull away. Right there, in a crowded jazz club, filled with strangers I'd never see again, Didi kissed me. It was an Olympic event and he went for gold, turning my initial resistance into breathless yearning. He slowly unlocked our lips, lit two cigarettes at the same time and handed me one *à la* Charles Boyer.

It occurred to me that the French were much more direct in their approach to sexuality than us Americans. Ever since Arthur made it clear that there was nothing I could say or do to recapture his ardor, I had felt invisible, *old* at thirty-seven. It was as if I could sashay down Broad Street wearing nothing but a feather boa and high heels and no one would take notice. But in the short time I had been in France, I not only felt visible, but *desired.* I enjoyed having men's eyes follow me like lazar beams. My age was irrelevant. So was my marital status, occupation and bank account. *Viva la france!*

Sex and politics, major no-no's at the American dinner table, were fair game in France, but discussing work and money was taboo. How refreshing! Before meeting Arthur, I can't tell you how many guys fanned out their credit cards on the first date in some bizarre financial mating dance. They talked, talked, talked about the gastric-bypasses, mergers and real estate deals they had done that day. More often than not, without ever asking a single question about me. By the end of the evening, I knew more about their assets than the IRS, how to perform a colonoscopy and everything that was wrong about their last girlfriend. And I do mean *everything*. That was what I feared most about the dissolution of my marriage, having to date again. Unless, of course, I started over in France. But not with Didi.

"That was nice but I have a boyfriend," I said.

The word "husband" didn't carry much weight, given the fact that I was practically sitting in Didi's lap and Arthur was on the other side of the ocean, in more ways than one.

"And you have a girlfriend," I continued. "Josie, at the hotel, she's really into you."

Didi shrugged, but took the bait.

"How do you know?" he asked.

"She told me you're the coolest guy in Mignon. The best kisser too. She's right about that."

"Josie said *that*? I haven't seen her in months."

Now it was my turn to shrug enigmatically. The musicians returned from their break and started in on *Take Five*. Didi bopped his head again but I could see the wheels turning. He wasn't thinking about me. He was thinking about Josie. Young, sweet, uncomplicated Josie.

32

"Late night?" Paul asked.

"Uh huh." My jaws unhinged in yet another extravagant yawn.

Didi had dropped me off at the hotel at three o'clock in the morning. I met Paul in the lobby at 9 a.m. Two cups of black coffee got my heart pumping but my brain was still in bed where my body longed to be. I headed toward Paul's car.

"I thought you wanted to go the *antiquité*," he said.

Right. I was curious about the Art Deco figurine in the window of the village antique shop. If it was within my range, I needed Paul to negotiate the price. I was incapable of haggling in French, or English for that matter. If a lava lamp at a yard sale was marked twenty dollars, it wasn't in my nature to offer fifteen.

Tibetan bells jingled as we entered *Daniel Brosseau, Antiquité & Brocante* which, like all antique shops worth their dust, was a dense maze of armoires, settees, Chinese screens, marble busts, chandeliers, military memorabilia and assorted *tchotchkes*. The shop was considerably larger that it appeared from the outside and I instinctively needed to investigate every nook and cranny, forgetting momentarily about the alabaster nymph. The owner, a gaunt man with bushy eyebrows and a silver goatee, paid no attention to us after the obligatory *bonjours*. Paul poked around African carvings and rain sticks while I wandered aimlessly amid the clutter, peering into Napoleonic cabinets and snuff boxes. I'm not a collector, except for vintage typewriters which I bought at church rummage sales until my home office looked like a repair shop. But I love the thrill of the hunt, the history and stories that lie dormant in these musty old artifacts of lives we'll never touch in any other way.

"*Alors*," said Paul, indicating that he had had enough.

I nodded and Paul nonchalantly asked the owner about the alabaster statue.

"Ah, you have a good eye," said Monsieur Brosseau. "*C'est tres charmant.*"

I feigned disinterest while the owner pointed out the qualities that justified it's price which was way out of my league. Paul sighed, thanked the owner and started to walk away.

"Monsieur?" Brosseau called after him.

Paul led me to the door.

"Wait, monsieur," the owner followed us practically outside.

A rapid volley ensued in French, too fast for me to follow. On both sides, there were fluttering hands, vaulted eyebrows, astonished expressions, blunt refusals and, finally, a firm shaking of hands.

"What just happened?" I asked as Paul followed Monsieur Brosseau to the counter.

"He came down in price by forty percent."

"How much is it in dollars?"

Paul's lips moved as he did the conversion.

"About two hundred and fifty, three hundred dollars. It's a good deal. Art Deco pieces like this in Toulouse go for twice as much. If you don't want it, I'll buy it."

Paul reached for his wallet.

"No, I want it." I said, flinging my VISA card on the counter as if it were a blackjack table.

If Arthur was deconstructing our marriage, it was time for me to start acquiring lovely things that gave my life new meaning and, if thrown, could do irrevocable damage. While Monsieur Brosseau wrapped the figurine, I looked at a stack of framed prints leaning against a wall. They looked familiar.

"I've seen these before," I said to Paul.

"Of course. Dali prints are everywhere."

"No, not just the prints. It's the matting and frames.

I picked up one of the smaller prints and carried it over to Monsieur Brosseau. "Excuse me, is this from the collection of Baron de Fondeville?"

Brosseau looked over the top of his glasses.

"*Oui, oui.* You also have a good eye, *mademoiselle*," he said. "I can give you an excellent price."

"No, no, thank you. I was just curious."

Paul sidled up to me.

"You're learning fast. Always pretend you're not interested."

"But I'm *not*. I just can't figure out how these prints survived the fire and, if they did, what they're doing here."

"Art collectors buy and sell all the time. It's an addiction. One of the more socially acceptable ones," Paul said.

I stifled a yawn.

"Where did you go last night?" he asked, using the same nonchalant tone as when he inquired about the figurine –as if he couldn't care less.

"To a jazz club in Marciac. *L'Atelier.*"

Paul tilted his head the way my cat Mongo does I offer him a lick of ice cream.

"All the way to Marciac on that little motorbike?"

So, Paul *was* watching last night.

"Yes. I enjoyed it."

Monsieur Bousseau handed me my credit card and a paper tote bag tied with ribbon containing the figurine, securely swathed in newspaper.

"You should be careful," Paul said, holding the door open.

I thought he was talking about my purchase.

"More people get killed on motorbikes than in wars," he said.

Look who's talking, Monsieur Lead Foot. I told Paul about my missing wedding ring and he agreed to lock the figurine in the trunk of his car for safe keeping, cushioning it with an old blanket he used for "*les piqueniques.*"

Our itinerary for that day included half a dozen armagnac vineyards. Just what I needed to clear my head. More booze. I climbed into the 2CV which, between you and me, was only marginally safer than Didi's motorbike and put on sunglasses so Paul couldn't tell I was nodding off.

"Where did you meet him?" Paul asked as we turned onto the main road.

"Who?"

"The guy with the Peugeot."

"At the village brasserie."

He drove in silence for few minutes, then spoke as if to himself.

"You should be careful."

33

Madame Picard was behind the reception desk wearing something I hadn't seen on her before. A pleasant smile.

"You are leaving tomorrow," she sang, "Here's your violet liqueur."

Oh, god. I had forgotten. She handed me a tall, slender purple bottle with a handwritten label. *Liqueur Violette de Château Mignon.* If it spilled in transit, it would ruin my clothes and damage my laptop. But such a pretty bottle. It would make a nice souvenir if I got rid of the contents and wrapped it in a towel. There are seven deadly sins and taking a hotel towel is *not* one of them. (When I was a child, we had so many hotel towels in our house that I thought our last name was Sheraton.)

Going up the stairs, I saw a vacuum cleaner in the hall. Josie was tidying up a guest room. She jumped when I stuck my head in the door.

"I need an extra towel," I said.

"*Un moment, mademoiselle.*" She pointed to the ceiling, indicating she would bring it to me.

Inside my room, I unscrewed the top and took a swig. *YUCK!* Sheila was right. It tasted like poison. As I poured it down the toilet, turning the water a lovely shade of lavender, I remembered what Paul had said. Nicole had a bottle in her purse. She drank it. He didn't. She was dead within hours. Maybe my poison lipstick theory was wrong. My gut instincts had led me astray before, like not realizing I was married to a gay man until he and his new partner registered at Williams Sonoma.

154

When Josie arrived with fresh towels, I thanked her and told her I had bumped into Didi at the brasserie.

"He misses you," I said.

"*Vraiment*? He said that?"

"Well, not exactly. He's too cool to admit it. But I could tell."

A light came on in Josie's eyes that I hadn't seen before. It was hope.

I had promised Paul that my time with him would be "strictly business." But I hadn't said anything about what I would do on my own. He had his dinner plans. I had mine. I called the reception desk and asked if Monsieur Picard was available for a brief interview. Madame said he was out and would not be back for another hour or two. That was all the time I needed. I called Sheila's room.

"*Bonjour,*" a silky voice purred.

I thought I had reached the wrong room.

"Sheila?"

"*C'est moi!*"

It's Fedora. You're French is improving."

"That's because I have a very good instructor. *Eel ay tray bone.* You remember Jean Pierre?"

"The policeman who took you to dinner?"

"And breakfast...." Her voice had a new lilt in it.

"Listen, Sheila, I'd love to hear all about it, but I need a favor."

"Shoot."

* * * *

I went back down to the lobby with a notepad and interviewed Madame Picard about her secret recipe for violet liqueur. As planned, our conversation was interrupted by a call from Sheila. With a sigh of exasperation and much annoyance, Madame put the phone back on its receiver.

"I am sorry but I must go to a guest's room. I won't be but a minute."

Make that twenty, I thought as Madame hobbled up the stairs. No one else was in the lobby. I slipped behind the reception desk to the door leading to the Picards' private apartment. It was open. What was I looking for? Anything that would link the Madame or Emile Picard to the murder. If Nicole had been blackmailing Guy de Fondeville, she might've been putting the squeeze on Picard too. Even if Nicole hadn't blackmailed Picard, Madame Picard might've put Nicole's pregnancy together with her husband and decided to take matters into her own hands.

Their apartment was set up like a hotel suite with a parlor, two bedrooms and two baths. At a glance, it was clear Madame and Monsieur Picard slept in separate rooms. Hers was festooned with sepia tinted photos of dead people, porcelain figurines and needlepoint pillows. His was as austere as a monk's cell. A bed, bookcase, bureau, lamp, devoid of sentiment. Picard slept here, but it wasn't where he *lived.* He probably maintained a *pied a terre* in Toulouse where his *matinées* had nothing to do with cinema, not an uncommon arrangement in France where discretion is prized over morals.

What I found was unexpected and puzzling. In a bureau drawer, underneath Madame Picard's uninspiring lingerie, was a large, black velvet jewelry box. Inside was a jumble of antique and contemporary jewelry that seemed incongruous with Madame Picard's shapeless dresses, bulky cardigans and sensible shoes. Diamond earrings, strands of pearls, cameos, a square cut emerald ring. I took a closer look at a diamond watch. It was Sheila's.

I heard footsteps coming my way. I stuffed the jewelry back inside the box, closed the bureau drawer and looked desperately for an escape route. I ruled out the closet and bathroom: whomever was coming could discover me by flinging open a door. I crawled under the bed. Not easy to do with my injured arm but, thankfully, the bed was high off the ground, leaving ample room for me and my sling. The bedroom door opened and Madame Picard's orthopedic shoes plodded across the Oriental carpet. She walked into the bathroom, sat on the toilet and dropped her panties.

Mercifully, my view didn't go higher than her heavily-veined calves. The toilet flushed. Water ran. Madame Picard came back into the bedroom and stood in front of her bureau for a few wrenching moments. Don't open it, I prayed. The drawer creaked open. Madame Picard screamed and fell back on the bed. The mattress sagged under her weight, enveloping me in a cloud of dust. I sneezed. Madame Picard's face appeared, upside down. This time, our screams were in unison. I crawled out from under the bed. Madame clutched her heart and backed away.

"Don't be afraid," I said.

Her eyes darted from me to her jewelry box and back again.

"I didn't take anything," I assured her.

"What do you want from me?" she whimpered like a frightened child.

A rather strange response to finding someone under your bed. Why wasn't she yelling for help? There was the phone. Why didn't she call the police? She chewed her lower lip.

"You want it? You can have it. Take all of it," she said, shoving the jewelry box toward me. "It has only brought me bad luck."

"I don't want your jewelry." I said.

"But you want *this*," she said, rummaging through her baubles and holding up a braided platinum band. My wedding ring!

Thank you, Grandmom, I thought, staring at the ring in disbelief and joy. Madame Picard rubbed her arms as if she were freezing, even though she wore a bulky sweater and the apartment was quite warm.

"Monsieur Picard must never know," she said, fingering a strand of pink pearls.

"If Nicole wasn't stealing, why did you fire her?"

"Someday Emile will leave me for a younger woman. *C'est la vie*," she said bitterly. "But it will not be for that *salope* Nicole."

The pearl necklace broke in her wrinkled hands, scattering on the floor.

"Now see what you've done?" she cried.

Madame Picard got down on her knees. The pearls were all over the place. I kneeled down beside her and helped gather them up.

"Monsieur Picard must never know," she repeated.

Madame wanted confidentiality from me and I wanted something from her.

"You moved Nicole's body didn't you?" I asked.

Her watery gray eyes studied mine, as if assessing to what extent I could be trusted.

"Yes, but it wasn't what you think."

"Then tell me."

She sat down on her bed, folded her hands like a schoolgirl and lowered her eyes. I reminded myself that this was once Vichy, France where the ability to keep a secret made the difference between life and death.

"I grew up in this chateau, you know. Turning my home into a hotel was not always pleasant. Every morning, before the day begins, I walk around the garden. It gives me a feeling of serenity. That horrible morning, I was out with the dogs and I found Nicole in the garden by the pool. She was dead. What could I do? I was frightened, but also worried about my guests. If someone looked out a window they would've seen her."

"I was afraid to call the police, because of my guests, you understand. But I had to do something. I dragged her behind a hedge and covered her with leaves. When you knocked on our door, I panicked. I forced my husband to move the body to the freezer in the chateau basement, then later to the field. It was my idea, not my Emile's."

Madame Picard took a deep breath and sighed.

I started to slide my wedding ring over my finger, then stopped and added it to the jumble of good luck charms hanging around my neck. Wearing it on my left hand would be false advertising.

* * * *

"Oh, my GAWD! Where did you find it?" Sheila gasped, hooking the vintage watch around her plump wrist.

"Madame Picard found it…. mixed up with the bed linens," I said.

No need to go into detail about Madame's kleptomania. Sheila was in unusually good spirits due to the attentions of the young policeman whom she referred to as her "French instructor."

"It's your last night," she said, "If you don't have plans, why don't you join Jean Pierre and me for dinner? He'll invite a friend. It will be a double date."

"I'd love to, but I have to work to do."

I did have to work. But not the kind Sheila imagined.

34

A taxi was out of the question. I needed a discreet driver this time, one that who would not tip off the police. I burrowed my face into Didi's neck to escape the muck spitting up from the wet road.

"I'll wait here," Didi said, turning off his bike's engine in the courtyard of Château des Rêves.

"No, you won't. You'll go home. I'll call you when I'm done. "

"Suppose someone comes?"

"They'll find me. Not you. Now go."

Didi fixed me with a brooding look, then gunned his bike and roared into the night. Someday that look would stop a woman's heart. There was not a single light inside or outside the château. I used my flashlight to slice through the darkness. The key to the cellar was where Jacques said it would be. The door opened to a narrow flight of cement stairs without a guard rail. I felt along the wall for a light switch. Finding none, I picked my way carefully down the stairs. Something cold and slithery grazed my face. I swatted at it with both hands. When it stopped moving, I realized I was engaged in combat with a beaded metal chain. I yanked it and, *voila,* the lights went on. Strategically placed bulbs created small pools of light every thirty feet or so, between caverns of looming darkness.

Water dripped. *Plop. Plop. Plop.* Cellars spook me. They speak of the grave. When I was a kid, I held my breath whenever I went down to the basement of my grandparents' house. Heavily framed photos of ancestors with startled expressions glowered from the walls

I had thought that the rough hewn table and chairs that served as Jacques' office were just a short distance from the entrance. Now I wasn't so sure. In every direction endless rows of barrels stood like silent sentinels. I had no clear memory of the layout. All I recognized was the color of the barrels which deepened from light tan to amber and emitted an increasingly pungent aroma the closer I got to Jacques' little corner. I followed my nose more than my eyes. A high-pitched squeak stopped me. Mice.

There, at last, was Jacques' nook with its worn table and meager supplies. A pouch of tobacco and rolling papers. Matches. An overflowing ash tray, as if he had just gone out to check on his vines. I sat down and felt under the table for the key to the storage room. The key was one of those old-fashioned jobs and it took a lot of jiggling and messing with the knob to turn the latch. The door opened with a low groan. The light switch was where it should be, to the right of the door.

The storage room was around ten feet by ten feet, with wooden shelves floor to ceiling, every shelf filled with paintings, prints and engravings. The Baron's complete art collection was there, including the lascivious nude that had hung on his bedroom wall. If the fire was insurance fraud, as the hidden art work suggested, Jacques was not an arsonist. But that did not vindicate him of Nicole's murder. And how did he know what was in the storage room if he was in Spain?

I wished I could talk to Arthur. He was a genius at understanding the criminal mentality. His motto was, "Murder is the logical outcome of an illogical mind."

I closed the storage room, put the key on its hook under Jacques' table and called Didi on my cell phone. Couldn't get a signal in the cellar. I climbed back up the cellar stairs and pushed the door open. Something pushed back.

"Didi?" I called out.

The door flew open and two black gloved hands shoved me backwards, down the cement stairs. I landed hard. Pain shot through my tailbone. Red lizard stilettos were level with my eyeballs. I followed them up, up, up a pair of black stockings to a white bouclé

Chanel suit, the jacket of which was festooned with gold chains and ropes of pearls the size of grapes. The face was in shadow but I would know that giraffe physique anywhere. Sandrine. Something glinted in her hand. It was the snub nose of a Baby Browning 25 automatic. One of those pretty little, pearl-handled numbers that could pass for a cigarette lighter.

"That's adorable. Did it come with matching earrings?" I said.

I get cute when I'm scared shitless.

"Get up," she ordered.

When I didn't move fast enough, Sandrine prodded me with her shoe.

"HEY! Watch it! You could put an eye out with that thing."

Painfully, I lifted myself into a sitting position. Everything hurt from the top of my head to the tip of my coccyx. Especially my coccyx.

"GET UP!" she shouted, waving her little pistol. "*VITE. VITE.*"

I couldn't do anything fucking *vite.*

"I think I broke something. Call an ambulance," I moaned.

"If I make a call it will be to the police. We have laws here in France."

Slowly, I managed to stand up, cradling my elbow with my other arm.

"Laws?" I muttered, "How many laws did you break setting the fire?"

I moved toward the stairs. Slowly.

"The other way. To the back," she said, pointing toward the storage room.

Having tagged along on undercover drug busts, I knew a thing or two about dealing with whackos with guns. RULE NUMBER ONE: KEEP THEM TALKING. As long as they're talking, they're not shooting. Narcissists like Sandrine always have something to say, especially when the subject is themselves.

When we reached Jacques' table, I crumpled into a chair. If Sandrine wanted me to go inside that storage room, she would have to carry or drag me there. My family always accused me of being "theatrical" and this was the time to make the most of my acting skills.

"*Merde.* Get up. Get up," Sandrine said, shaking me by the shoulder.

RULE NUMBER TWO: DO NOT LET THEM LEAD YOU TO A SECLUDED PLACE.

I didn't budge. True, she could pop off a round into my head, but I was betting she wouldn't want to risk getting blood splatter on her dry-clean-only ensemble. She walked a few feet away. I heard water running, then the *click click click* of her heels coming back. For an instant, I thought Sandrine had an ounce of compassion. She was getting me a glass of water. Maybe an aspirin.

"JESUS!" I screamed as she poured the water over my head.

"WHAT THE FUCK YOU DO THAT FOR?"

Now I wasn't just in pain. I was soaking wet and angry.

"Get in there," she ordered, pointing toward the storage room.

"NO!"

"I am telling you. GO! I have a gun."

"Yeh? And I have a fucking headache! You want to shoot me? Do it and get it over with."

Her upper lip twitched. Maybe the gun wasn't loaded. Then again. RULE NUMBER THREE: BE EMPATHETIC. IT'S ALWAYS ABOUT THEM.

"I'm sure you had a good reason for what you did," I said. "Your husband was unfaithful."

"Unfaithful? You think I don't know about Guy's little adventures? Seducing the Baron does not require much skill, as you know," she sniffed, "And I had nothing to do with the fire. It was Guy's idea. He had financial difficulties. I never involve myself with those matters. I understand that in your country wives take an interest in such things. I believe the expression is *wearing the pants.*"

"Financial problems?" I asked, "Excuse my French, but you live in a fucking château. You drive a Jaguar. You probably spent more on those shoes than I make in a month."

Sandrine shook her silken mane. "You think only the poor have problems? The more money you have, the bigger the problems."

"Can't wait to find out."

"The Baron has expensive habits. What he didn't spend on art, he left on the roulette tables in Biarritz."

"Why are you so vindictive?" I prodded. "Your husband loved you and Nicole could've been your daughter."

"My daughter?" The blood drained from Sandrine's face. "What do you know about my daughter?"

35

"When I was 15, I had dreams, the same dreams as all poor country girls, a cliché really, to go to the Riviera and be 'discovered.' I was discovered quickly enough by the hotel manager, a man my father's age. Married, of course. I was pregnant. They took the baby from me before I could hold her in my arms and gave her to a family without telling me their name or address. They said it would be easier that way.

"A few years later, when my face was on the cover of every magazine, I started getting letters from Marseilles. I knew what they wanted. I didn't care. I had money. What I didn't have was a child and, by that time, a doctor had told me I would never have another. At the beginning, I sent lavish gifts. Little couture dresses, fur coats, expensive dolls. Then just checks. That's what they really wanted. In return, I got a Christmas card every year with a photo of a beautiful, blond angel named Nicole. My Nikki.

"Were they taking advantage? Probably. I didn't care. It gave me a certain peace. But then, about four years ago, the letters stopped. I felt a sense of loss I cannot explain. Then, last year, she arrived. She was the right age, the right hair color and spoke with a Marseilles accent. She said her name was Nicole. I thought, is it possible? Could it be? My daughter has come to me at last.

"The illusion lasted only a few days. I saw through her quickly enough. She was very clever. She never *said* she was my daughter, but she knew things only my daughter would know. I gave her a job, clothes, money. The Baron and I disagreed on this matter, but I insisted. Then she went too far. *Comprenez?* "

"You mean sleeping with the Baron?" I said.

"*Pfttttt*," Sandrine blew out a puff of air. "Infidelity does not destroy a marriage. It invigorates it. No, no, what that *putain* did was much worse. She said she was going to have the Baron's child. I offered to pay for her abortion if she would go back to Marseilles. Instead of going away, she set a trap for Jacques. You see, she didn't just want money. She wanted to ruin my *name*. You Americans can't possibly understand because you don't have names. You only have money. "

Sandrine was breathing hard, reliving her anger and rage. She reached for a bottle of Armagnac and poured herself a glass, placing the gun on the table. I maintained eye contact and pretended not to notice.

"I knew she was a fraud, an extortionist. I threatened to call the police if she didn't go away," Sandrine continued. "That's when she told me my daughter was dead. Killed in a car accident four years ago, when the letters stopped. It's as if she murdered my Nikki right in front of my eyes."

"You just said your daughter died in a car accident. How was Nicole responsible?"

Sandrine's voice was barely a whisper.

"Nicole was driving."

There is no death penalty in France. Nicole was a drug dealer, a blackmailer and an adulteress. Sandrine was a member of the aristocracy. A criminal defense lawyer might add that Madame de Fondeville was under the influence of Didrex. The court would be sympathetic. But not if she also had murdered her husband.

"You were in a state of shock," I said, "You did not intend to murder anyone. Not Nicole, not your husband. It was an accident."

"Accident?" Sandrine's face contorted into a grimace. "There are no accidents. There are just bad decisions, like Nicole's decision to blackmail me and your decision to come here tonight." She gripped the gun with one hand and reached into her purse with the other.

"Put this on," she said. It was a lipstick.

"Uh, no thanks."

Her finger cocked the trigger. I heard a scraping sound. I was hoping it was Paul.

"PUT IT ON!" she shouted.

"Why? Are you afraid to shoot me with that toy gun?"

Sandrine's eyes narrowed and her mouth turned into a hard, thin red line. She squeezed the trigger and fired off a round. *BLAM!* A bottle of armagnac exploded behind me.

"Now do as I say," she ordered.

I put on the lipstick with a shaking hand. Sandrine poured another shot of brandy.

"Drink this. All of it," she ordered. "It will work faster that way. You will feel nothing but your heart racing until it stops. A delicious death."

I took a big swig but didn't swallow. Having grown up with five siblings, my projectile marksmanship was world class. I spit the brandy right in her eye. The dark brown armagnac dribbled down Sandrine's cheek onto her white Chanel jacket. She screamed so loud she must've paid retail. I rubbed my mouth with my sleeve to remove the lipstick and kicked Sandrine hard just below the knees. She fell to the cement floor and howled again.

It wasn't a fair match. I was wearing Doc Martens. She was in Louboutin stilettos. I grabbed a chunk of Sandrine's perfect hair to get her attention, then stomped on her hand until released the gun. I picked up the gun and ran for the exit. A large animal with its eyes on fire came out of the shadows. It was Jacques. He ran toward Sandrine. I thought he was going to kill her, instead he knelt down and cradled her like a child.

* * * *

I limped out into the moonlit courtyard. There, among the shadowy figures, police cars and ambulance was the one person I did not expect to see.

"*Paul?*"

He pulled me to his chest and squeezed so tight I couldn't breathe.

"How did you…?"

"I saw you get on the motorbike," he mumbled into my hair.

"You *followed* me?"

He released me just enough so that I could see the quizzical expression on his face.

"If anything happened to you, I wouldn't get paid."

Even in my rattled state, I knew he was lying. He followed me because he was *jealous*. Hot damn. The Santeria spell worked!

"I didn't see your car following us." I said.

"I drove with the lights off and parked in the woods. I saw Sandrine arrive. When I heard the gun shot, I called the police. I didn't know if you were…" his voice trailed off.

All eyes turned towards the cellar door as Jacques emerged with Sandrine, pale and limp in his arms like a dying swan. She wasn't seriously injured, just a fractured fibia, but she played it for all it was worth. After she was whisked away in an ambulance, Beaumonde turned to me with the weariness of man who had just climbed the 1,665 stairs of the Eiffel Tower only to discover he could've taken the elevator.

"The tests on the lipstick came back positive for nitroglycerin," he snapped. "It can be fatal in itself, but when combined with alcohol, it is lethal."

"Does that mean that Sandrine de Fondeville will be charged with her husband's murder?" I asked.

Beaumonde rocked on his heels.

"The Baron's death was ruled as a heart attack, no doubt triggered by the nitroglycerin and alcohol in his bloodstream. But it remains unclear if there was intent to kill." Beaumonde took a deep gulp of the chilly night air. "I have just one request, *Mademoiselle*."

"Yes?"

"Go home."

Paul looped a protective arm around my shoulder and guided me to his car.

"What was that about?" he asked.

"Sandrine poisoned a lipstick with nitroglycerin, then gave it to Nicole. It would've killed her eventually, but the night Nicole was with you, she drank heavily which accelerated the toxins. She almost succeeded in killing me the same way."

"The Inspector said something about Baron de Fondeville having a heart attack," Paul said.

"You know, Paul, I really wasn't following what the Inspector was saying. My back hurts."

Someday, I might share a good laugh with Paul about Fondeville's penchant for cosmetics and what I was doing with him the night he died. Someday when Hell freezes over.

"What I can't figure out is why Jacques was so protective of Sandrine. She was ready to hang the fire and murders on him. He knew it," I said.

"Jacques is a true Gascon. His allegiance isn't to the Fondevilles, it's to the land."

Paul probably had a point. If given a chance, Jacques would nurse his charred vineyard back to life. It was just as well. They'll never make a decent Armagnac in California.

36

Paul and I stood on Toulouse's Pont Neuf Bridge watching barges glide along *Le Canal du Midi.*

"You dropped something," he said.

I looked down and saw the piece of paper on which I had written Paul's name to cast the Santeria spell. Paul bent to pick it up. I beat him to it.

"It's just a list of things I want to do in Toulouse." I said, quickly tucking the note into my pocket. "The canal was at the top of my list."

"When I was a child, I was obsessed with it," Paul said. "My teachers called it by its other name, *Le Canal des Deux Mers.* The idea that this narrow body of water connected the Atlantic Ocean and the Mediterranean Sea fascinated me. I must've drawn a thousand pictures of it. My dream was to build a little boat and sail across France from one sea to the other."

"Did you?"

"It's still in the planning stages."

Paul gazed longingly at the colorful barges with fanciful names – *San Souci, Mirage, Petite Fleur* - moving below. At that moment, I caught a glimpse of him as a child choosing just the right color crayon for his ship's sails.

Exploring Toulouse with Paul on my last day in France was bittersweet. *La Cité Rose*, as it is called for its pink basilicas and palaces, had everything I adored about Paris, but on a more intimate scale in a sunny, semi-tropical climate. Unexpected little parks, sidewalk cafes, Baroque architecture, flea markets and throngs of university students, a necessary ingredient to keep a city vibrant and stimulating. I could live here, I thought. This idea was reinforced by the fact that my favorite Parisian department store, Galeries Lafayette, had a branch in Toulouse.

"Souvenirs," I pleaded.

Paul was understanding as I dashed around the first floor of Galeries Lafayette, scooping up gifts for family and friends. Scarves, earrings, handbags. I'll never find these in the States, I thought, grabbing tights patterned with butterflies in aubergine, teal and chocolate. I bought a perfume, *Eau Belle*, because Paul said it smelled like summer and the bottle was shaped like me, curvy on top and bottom.

Although I had had my fill of churches, I trouped along to *Basilique Saint-Sernin,* the largest Romanesque church in the west and made the appropriate oohs and aahs. Paul sensed my disinterest and we headed off to the Museum of Contemporary Art which was located in a former slaughter house. Ouch.

* * * *

"You are going to start a new fashion craze," Paul said.

He was referring to the sling I had fashioned out of my scarf. My arm and back were responding well to a combination of immobilization, codeine and champagne. Two out of three were doctor's orders. Dinner that night was a moveable feast aboard *Le Papillon*, a restaurant barge. The domes and rooftops of Toulouse drifted by at a languid pace. The canal was just wide enough for two barges to pass, flanked on either side by towering oaks whose autumn leaves formed a golden canopy.

We dined on baby artichokes, foie gras, smoked salmon, duck magret, leek tarts, a salad of pears and Roquefort and, of course, Patis Gascon, drizzled with Armagnac. Paul cut my food for me. I was a happy invalid. After dinner, we didn't walk to Paul's studio on Place Victor Hugo. We floated. As I recall, Paul never asked if I wanted to go to my hotel or back to his place. He merely laced his fingers in mine and murmured, "*Ça va?*"

His spacious loft was a third floor walk-up, half photography studio, half living space, divided by a translucent glass screen that softly changed colors. The décor conveyed minimalist sensibilities black lacquered floors, white walls, black leather and chrome furniture and books everywhere. On glass shelves, stacked on tables, on the floor. There wasn't a Mao poster or futon in sight.

"I have a confession," he said once we were in his apartment.

Here it comes, I thought. He's bi, married or wants to try on my pantyhose.

"I have never been to the United States. In fact, I've never traveled outside the Continent."

That's it?

"I would love to work with you again," he continued. *"C'est possible?"*

I burst out laughing.

"What is it? I said something wrong?" Paul asked.

"No, no. I was just thinking. We make a good team."

"Maybe I come to *Noo York* or *Feeladelphia*?"

A trace of a smile played across his lips. I followed him with my eyes as he went in search of more bubbly. Paul gave me my third class of champagne. Or was it my fourth? He kicked off his shoes and put a Claude Nougaro disk on the CD player.

Dansez sur moi, Dansez sur moi, Le soir de vos fiançailles, Dansez dessus mes vers luisants, Comme un parquet de Versailles...

"Dance with me," he said.

"But my arm..."

"Dansez sur moi," he crooned.

We danced carefully around the room, my arm in its sling.

"I thought you don't like making love to a woman who has had too much to drink."

"There are exceptions."

The End

www.ingramcontent.com/pod-product-compliance
Lightning Source LLC
LaVergne TN
LVHW011812030225
802815LV00028B/430